Together . . .
Always and Forever?!

Together . . .
Always and Forever?!

Avani Vora

PARTRIDGE
A Penguin Random House Company

To order additional copies of this book, contact
Partridge India
000 800 10062 62
orders.india@partridgepublishing.com

www.partridgepublishing.com/india

This debut novel of mine is dedicated to the world's most amazing parents, Amul and Aparna Vora. Without your support and love, this book would not have been possible. Love you so much . . .

Acknowledgements

Firstly, I would really like to thank you for picking up my book. It really means the world to me.

There are a lot of people whose hard work goes into the publishing and making of this book. My overwhelming and loving gratitude to my parents, without whom, Aisha and her journey of love would not have come alive.

Secondly, I would like to thank my little sister Asmi for all the love and care, for always being there in my good times as well as bad, and for instilling strength into me when I desperately needed it. Thank you so much, my ray of hope.

Next, I would like to thank my badminton coach, Sir Ravi Kunte, for the unbelievable guidance, support, and love he has showered on me throughout the years. Thank you so much, sir, my mentor, my guide, for always being there for me.

Next in line are two people whose amazing feedback has helped me throughout and whose love has kept me going. To my first editors and my soul sisters, Tejaswini Potdar and Abha Dasgupta, love you lots and loads. I would also like to thank Pranay, Tanmay, Devaki, Pranita, Samruddhi, and my cousins Aditi, Aditya, Jay, and Yash for inspiring me in ways more than one and for always believing in me when I lost faith in myself.

A colossal thank you to all the teachers from my school, especially Miss Shubhangi Dalal and Miss Supriya, who have moulded me into the person that I am now. Thank you so much. I would also like to thank all my teachers in symbiosis for their support.

A heartfelt gratitude to Partridge Publishing for publishing my book and a special thank you to all the members on the team—Tony Myers, Gemma Ramos, Rey Flores, Marie Giles et al.—for all their efforts and hard work. This book would not have been what it is without you guys.

Lastly, I want to thank everyone who has believed in me and who has been there for me throughout this wonderful journey. If I have forgotten any names, please do forgive me.

Thank you so much to you, the reader, who bought my book. I would love hearing back from you about the book as I would surely use the knowledge and tips you will provide in the near future to enrich my writing and improve it.

Thank you once again.

Yours,

Avani Vora

Chapter 1

'I think I should get going now,' I said, taking a deep breath.

'I am gonna miss you so much, Aisha,' exclaimed Eva.

'I am gonna miss you too, Eva. The past five years were more beautiful than I could have asked for,' I said, getting emotional now.

All those memories had started brimming up in my chest, and a small sob was trying to escape my mouth. I couldn't believe I was actually leaving Paris. It had become somewhat my home, to be frank, rather than my second home. I grew up in this city; this city had moulded me in my growing years into a mature, independent, and a comparatively stronger person than who I was before leaving India.

'Do you wanna miss your flight, babe?' asked Eva, breaking into my thoughts and making me aware I was running late on my schedule.

'Nope . . . Was just reminiscing the past and was having a last look at the beauty and glory of Paris. But I knew I had to leave one day. It seems like I just arrived though . . .' I moaned sorrowfully.

'Yeah right! Now don't make me emotional and get your ass off our flat, which is very soon gonna be *my* flat,' squeaked Eva, being her usual outgoing self.

1

Laughing, we both left. She dropped me at the airport, and that was probably the last time I was seeing her for some years at the least. We hugged each other goodbye and promised to keep in touch.

The flight back home was long and disturbing, which was obvious given the fact that Jay kept popping in my dreams. Jay . . . I really don't know where to start or what label to give to the relationship we share. It is something definitely matchless and very special. Something more than friendship, on my part at least, but I wasn't able to pinpoint exactly what it is.

He was one person who understood me more than anyone else. Especially after Dad's death under mysterious conditions he was the only one I opened up to. He was my go–to person in any case. Guys badgering me, fights with Mom (in which, in fact, he was the negotiator), troubles in college, or even dilemmas solving a math problem—the first person I turned to was Jay. I had missed him all these years, and when I am finally going to meet him, I am all afraid and nervous, with reasons being unknown.

The flight landed, and I went through all the customs and the checks. There waiting for me outside the airport was my mom. I had missed her all these years. My relationship with my mom is quite intricate and complicated. It is quite contradictory to what they show on those daily soaps. Though we don't really have that perfect relationship, we love each other, but we cannot stay together for more than five minutes without fighting and arguing.

None of my friends knew I was coming back, so I didn't even expect to see anyone else other than Mom.

'It's so good to see you. I still don't get why you couldn't come home in the vacations for the past *three years*!' she said with a clear hint of annoyance in her voice and stressing very particularly on the last two words.

'The plane tickets had become thrice as costly, and I had a lot of work in there, Mom' I tried reasoning with her.

'Don't give me silly reasons now. Let's just leave it. Let's get you home first, you are a mess,' she said, heaving a sigh.

Maybe she knew the reason that I didn't come home for three years. Now it had been three years since Dad's death, and my obduracy to come to India was pretty evident, I guess, because everything in India—every small thing in here—reminded me so much about him. I have spent sixteen years of my life with him over here; I have spent sixteen years of my life loving him over here.

'How are we going home?' I asked.

'Didn't I tell you Jay has come too?' she asked, confused whether she had mentioned it or not.

'What? Jay? Really?' I exclaimed with astonishment and a tinge of excitement, clearly exulted with the knowledge.

'Yeah, he is waiting by the car perhaps. He wanted to give us some privacy, he said! Sweet boy he is,' she said, going into her own thoughts.

Mom adored Jay. But then, why wouldn't she? After all, he was the perfect son one could ever ask for—excellent at studies, a state-level basketball player, the head of the fine arts department in high school as well as in college, full of manners, ethics, and philosophy, and respectful to anyone and everyone. A typical showpiece, isn't he? A guy anyone would be proud to call as a friend, a boyfriend, a son, etc.

I was so eager to meet him! Five years had gone by since we had last seen each other as he himself had gone to the States for higher studies, and we were just seventeen then for crying out loud. I bet he must have changed in all these years.

We entered the parking lot, and there I saw him leaning on our Ford, in deep thoughts. He was taller than the last time I had seen him. He must easily be six feet. His muscles had welled up; his hair, the same shade of brown even now— all distorted in different directions, which kinda looked sexy and endearing. He turned around, and I swear to God it was the most utterly and breathtakingly beautiful face I had ever seen, with those grey eyes, which make me go frail, and that half-dimpled smile, which still causes butterflies in my stomach. If I had to describe Jay then he was that typical 'poster guy'. He was exceptionally good-looking, tall, proportionately muscular, fair, with grey eyes, and with the additional bonus of a half dimple on his left cheek.

'Oh, Lord God! Just look at you! Someone has really changed. You have become more beautiful than the last time I saw you!' he said notoriously, winking at me.

'Change is positive in the guy standing in front of me too! Wonder why people don't keep mirrors at their place!' I said, pulling his leg.

'Ah!' he said, running his hand through his hair. 'So even you pull my leg now? Great!'

He looked into my eyes intensely, but then realizing Mom was nearby, he put my luggage in the back seat, and getting into the driver's seat, he said, 'I have, um, bought something for you.' He stepped out of the car again.

'For me?' I asked, confirming, a little amazed and overwhelmed by his thoughtfulness. 'Oh! That's really considerate of you,' I exclaimed, breaking into a smile.

He pressed a gift-wrapped box into my hands, and with fervent zeal in his eyes, he said, 'Open it. I just hope you like it.'

The fact that he thought so much for me made my day. Wondering what it contained, I carelessly tore the gift wrap in a hurry and opened the box. Inside the box was a heart-shaped pendant with a picture of us together in it.

I was stunned into silence. I couldn't believe he still remembered my obsession for pendants, and it had a picture of us—us together. I just stood there, silent. I could hear Mom talking to somebody on the phone nearby.

Breaking the silence between us, he said, 'I can get it changed if you don't like it,' fearing that my craze for such pendants had waned off. I didn't say anything, but tears were starting to well up in my eyes.

'Hey, what's wrong?' he asked worriedly, panicking a bit.

I just hugged him. I hugged him tight. We could hear Mom coming back from the arena she had gone to so as to catch some signal as she was talking on the phone.

'We need to get going, Ash,' he said, sensing the urgency of the moment.

'Yeah, I am, um, aware of it. I am really sorry. I, er, was in the flow of emotions. I just couldn't help it,' I said, realizing what I had done.

We both were kinda embarrassed or, putting it in a better way, had gone scarlet due to the sudden hug. Things used to be as easy as breathing between us before we both departed to our respective destinations for higher studies.

But now, maybe things were a bit different. With a lot of questions revolving in my head, I sat into the back seat of the car and slept due to exhaustion, fatigue, and jet lag.

The next few weeks went into rearranging my stuff, getting used to the Indian conditions again, socializing, and meeting old friends. I didn't really see much of Jay in those weeks except in friends' parties, wherein he chose to ignore me or let's say he was just too busy with his other 'girl friends' to even come and say hi to me. But there was this particular gal, Shanaya (whose name I came to know on further enquiry), who was seen with him 24/7. I don't know why, but I disliked this gal to the core of my heart without any particular reason, and I swear I hated her closeness to Jay. It was as if I had been replaced by her in his life, and that surely didn't go down too well with me. I had never felt this possessive over someone, not even over my apparent ex! I had dated a guy named Chris in Paris just to distract myself and also because he resembled Jay a lot, and this in itself was a premonition that what I felt for Jay was not limited to the likings of friendship. It was something beyond that.

There was this particular party at Kruttika's house. I was standing on the terrace which had a splendid view, and there was a zephyr blowing.

'The view from here is fabulous, isn't it?' said a voice coming from behind.

I knew exactly whose voice it was even without looking behind. I suddenly became conscious of my tangled hair, and straightening it, I replied, 'Yeah, it is. You have been here before, have not you?'

Moving towards me with a glass of wine, he said, 'Yep. Shanaya and Kruttika were the best of friends from the very beginning. Don't you remember?'

'I never knew Shanaya, but yeah, Kruttika was always a good friend. Though I knew that you and a gal named Aisha were best friends!' I choked, my voice breaking at the end.

'Huh? Where did that come from, Ash? You have a fallacy over here! You and I were always best friends and will always be!' he said with an agonized voice and also with a hint of annoyance.

'Yeah right, Jay! You don't even say hi to me when you see me. We go without talking for days, and there's this cold, icy distance between us which further makes us apart. And you call me your best friend, my foot!' I almost yelled at him with tears in my eyes.

'Now, now, Ash, take it easy,' he said, offering me a glass of wine. 'You haven't changed a bit, have you? It's the same old emotional and sensitive Aisha Mukherjee.'

'No thanks, I am a teetotaller, and I thought you knew me,' I said sarcastically, declining his drink. 'Yeah, it's the same old same Aisha again. Go to your new Shanaya.' I was angry and grimacing.

'I was, er, going to tell you about Shanaya,' he said, cautiously choosing his words.

There was a sudden noise of the opening of the door, and lo and behold, the devil appeared. Like they say, name the devil, and the devil is here.

'What are you doing up here, baby? I was looking for you all around the house,' she said with a typical high frilled girly tone.

Shanaya—the name itself was a giveaway to what she was. She was around five feet eight inches tall, with shiny straight black hair, which came down till her waist. She had a figure which matched the models on the cover pages of magazines, with pretty features, all symmetrical, and with a childish smile. She was just like those 'too good to be true' type of gals we see in famous paintings and carvings. She was downright hot, and she was gorgeously beautiful. She was a bad stab to my ego, to be blunt.

'I was talking to Aisha here. You remember? I told you about her,' Jay said, a little bit weary as if someone had given him a huge workload to complete on a Sunday.

'Not really. An introduction would perhaps help,' she said and positioned herself besides Jay, linking his arm with her arm.

Yeah right! Why will the bitch remember me! I thought disdainfully.

'All right!' he said, scratching his head. 'So, Shanaya, this is, um, Aisha, my best friend, the one who had gone to Paris whom I had told you about, and Ash, this is Shanaya, my . . . er . . . my g-girlfriend,' he said hesitatingly, faltering out the last word.

The last two words stung me like a bee's bite, and it felt as if an old rusting knife had been thrust into my intestines. It was a big blow for me—the introduction of the girlfriend and the realization that I still was deeply, madly, and irrevocably in love with the guy standing in front of me, my best friend! The realization hit me so hard that I collapsed, and the next thing I knew was that I was in someone's bedroom. I could hear soft murmurs, and I slowly opened my eyes to a dim and comforting yellow light.

'Are you all right?' Jay asked with genuine concern, and I could see anxiety in his eyes.

'I don't know. My head hurts,' I said with a weak and somewhat traumatized voice.

'I am dropping you home, and I want no arguments on that,' he said firmly as I was about to open my mouth to protest.

After that dead-serious look on his face, I murmured a meagre okay. He lifted me up, and that touch ignited a large number of firecrackers in my stomach. It was a short-lived dream. It was heaven, those two minutes from the room to the car. It was *my heaven*.

He put me down on the seat and secured my belt. He drove very meticulously and slowly, which was very unlikely of him as he loved speed.

'Why did you faint suddenly?' he asked out of curiosity and concern of course.

'I don't know,' I replied tersely, and my words were filled with loathe for the other gal.

'You seem to hate Shanaya, don't you?' he asked.

'Well, I don't hate her, but I particularly don't like her either,' I said, concealing my jealousy and hatred for her.

'Now that's a clever answer.' He chuckled. 'Now don't you give any pressure to that brain of yours, and go to sleep. It's gonna take time, given the distance, and I'll put you in once we reach,' he said softly and gently as if he were my guardian.

'Cool then. Thanks,' I said, half-smiling.

I loved the fact that he cared for me, and that somewhat gave birth to hope. With gleeful thoughts and Taylor Swift's

'Love Story' playing in the background, I slipped into a peaceful sleep.

I woke up the next morning to the loud chirping of the birds in our garden. Mom was feeding them grains, I guess. Planning to go to the kitchen to make myself some coffee, I went to the hall. I was about to step into the kitchen when I saw Jay sleeping peacefully on the large divan in the hall. He looked like a kid while sleeping—innocent, pure, and sweet—and that look brought a wide smile on my face as I was staring at him with adoration and awe.

'What are you beaming at?' enquired Mom, entering the house with a big empty bowl with some small grains still stuck on it.

'Nothing in particular. I was just reminded of something,' I said, still grinning like an idiot.

'Your reminiscence of whatever the thing is reminds me to ask you, why and how did you faint yesterday?' she asked still cheesed off and cross.

'Too much of parties these days and late nights, I guess,' I said, hoping she would ask me to refrain from going to the parties so that I could see no more of Shanaya and her fakery.

'This is the result of you not eating much! Look how thin you have become during your stay in Paris!' she ranted.

'I am *fit* now! I was *fat* before! There's a difference between an *a* and an *i*, Mom!' I disagreed with her, but then realizing that this was a never-ending argument, I decided to change the topic and said, 'Why is Jay sleeping here? Did he not go home?'

'Well, he came in, holding you in his arms. I panicked a bit, but he assured me all is well. He seemed very tired and weary, plus his condition couldn't be described as pleasant! So I asked him to spend the night in here,' she said, worrying about him too. My mom worries about everyone, I guess.

'So why is he sleeping on the divan and not in the spare bedroom?' I asked, craving for more details.

'I asked him to put you in your bedroom, and after he came back, he asked for a glass of water, but when I came back, he was sound asleep on the divan. I didn't wake him up, he seemed dead tired,' Mom said, taking a breath after filling me in with the details.

'As inquisitive as before,' said Jay in a kinda hoarse voice, his sleep disturbed due to the commotion caused by my and Mom's voices.

'Oh, I am very sorry! I didn't mean to wake you up!' I said in an apologetic tone, feeling kinda guilty.

'Are you better?' Mom asked him, giving him a glass of water. 'Freshen up till then, I will make you both hot coffee.'

'Yes, Auntie, nothing is wrong with me. It was your daughter who fainted yesterday,' he said, giving me that 'you better get better' look.

'It was just due to exhaustion! Now don't you go around making a whole sentence out of one single word! You are acting as if I have been diagnosed with swine flu or something!' I said, protesting in a repulsive manner.

'No point in arguing with her,' both Jay and Mom said at the same time.

Laughing, all three of us left for our respective destinations.

It was a great beginning to my day until that phone call. Jay was in the shower, and his phone was ringing. I picked it up. A female voice came from the other side.

'Baby, where have you been? You were supposed to pick me up from Kruttika's party last night! You never came back, plus you were not picking up your phone since yesterday night!' said the other gal, her tone demanding and dominating.

'Er, Jay is not here. May I know who this is? I'll convey the message if you want, or else call later,' I said politely.

'Who the hell are you? And what on God's hell are you doing with Jay's phone? I am his girlfriend, for your kindest information,' she said angrily and cynically.

'Oh! Er, Shanaya?' I asked.

'Yes, that's me! Who the heck are you? And where's Jay?' she said, bombarding me with her questions.

'Shanaya, um, this is Aisha here. We met last night, and as far as Jay's concerned, he is in the shower,' I said, trying to be as civil as possible.

'Whaaaat? Get one freaking thing straight in your head, shortie. Jay is *my* boyfriend, and you better stay away from him, as away as possible, or there will be no one worse than me!' she said, threatening me.

How dare she call me a shortie! That bitch! C'mon! I am not that short! I mean five feet and six inches is not short! But I guess she's just a brainless beauty! One more blondie!

'Even you get one thing straight then, you oblivious dork. Jay is my best friend, and I have known him all my life! I have more right on him than you do, so back off!' I said. Complacent with my reply, I banged the phone.

I didn't realize that Jay had come down till then. I felt like I had given one of the biggest giveaways of my feelings for him if he had heard the conversation, and from that smug smile on his face, it looked like he had.

'Ah! Two hot and beautiful gals fighting over me, I am soooo loving it!' he said, laughing loudly and his mirth shaking the whole table.

'What are you talking about? I-I, um, there's nothing like that!' I said, stumbling out my words.

'Yeah right, as if! You can fool everyone but me, Aisha Mukherjee! I know you too well for that!' he said mischievously, but there was deepness in his words.

It was true though. No one knew me as well as him. I had thought, after all these years, our bond must have hit the rocks, and the understanding must have gone down the well, but here I was being proven wrong. Fortunately for me, my mom came out of the kitchen with two steaming hot cups of coffee like a saviour for me!

'Here you go, kiddos, your coffee. Hot, steaming, and strong . . . just as you like it,' Mom said, satisfied with her job, and went to get her cup in the kitchen.

Taking advantage of the situation, Jay whispered in my ear, 'Don't ya think I will forget it. Oh, Lord! I love thee!' He chuckled, giving me a jovial look which irked me!

His voice was still ringing in my ears. We had our coffee, which did relax me as Mom had predicted, and he was about to leave.

'Thanks a ton, Auntie. That coffee just made my head a bit lighter!' he joked around.

'That's just temporary, *beta*! Aisha here will add to it again!' Mom said, pulling my leg, and both of them started laughing, which bugged me even more.

I despised the fact that Mom was pulling my leg in front of Jay! Why Jay of all the people! I sighed and went out to accompany Jay till the gate.

'Thanks for dropping me home yesterday. I really don't know what I would have done without you,' I said, expressing my gratitude towards him and appreciating his gesture.

He pulled me closer, and we were as close as never before, and I blushed, my cheeks pink, and I didn't have it in me to look up in his eyes because if I did, I feared he will decipher the intensity of my feelings for him.

Pulling myself away from him, I said in a sarcastic tone, 'Go to your Shanaya! She's waiting for you.'

'If I could just get the confirmation of your fee . . .' his voice trailed off, and he left the sentence incomplete.

'You want a confirmation of what, Jay? What are you talking about?' I asked out of curiosity and interest of course.

'Nothing, I got to go. As you mentioned earlier, Shanaya must be waiting for me!' he said, and there was a typical edge to his tone, and I could sense sarcasm in his words. He left, leaving me in a string of thoughts, or you can say *questions* for that matter.

What did he mean by that? Why did he pull me so close to him, and what confirmation was he talking about? What does that mean? What does he wanna prove, or is it that he actually has feelings for me? But there would be no Shanaya if he would have feelings for me, would there? There were endless number of questions in my head which I had no answers to, and I had no clue as to how I was ever gonna get those answers. There was just one person who could answer all these questions, and he just left me hopeless around five minutes ago, leaving me confused about his feelings and showing me two completely contradictory sides of himself within a span of just five freaking minutes.

I couldn't stop thinking about the noon incident. His eyes said a different story from what his words conveyed. Why are guys so hard to make out? Is it necessary for them to complicate things so much? Huh! Guys will be guys! Bunch of assholes! Engrossed in my thoughts, I dozed off on the couch itself! I woke up to my Fefe's 'Stuttering' ringtone.

'Hello?' I said in somnolent tone.

'Um, hello, can I talk to Aisha?' a female voice said from the other side.

The voice sounded somewhat familiar! Ugh! I couldn't make out who she was though.

'Yeah, this is Aisha here. Is this, by any chance, Abha?' I asked, guessing randomly. I thought her to be Abha because she had the same velvety texture to her voice!

'Oh, wow! I can't believe you recognized me!' she said, astounded and somewhat flattered.

'Ha ha! Your voice is still the same. So what's up? How did you get my number though?' I asked, surprised that she had my number. Very few people had my Indian number.

'Jay, of course!' she said as if I had asked her some silly question like 'Is Taj Mahal one of the wonders of the world?'

'Oh yeah, right, I didn't think about that!' I said. *Why does Jay have to be everywhere in my world?* I thought ironically.

'Anyways, I called to invite you for a movie tomorrow evening. Will you be able to make it?' she asked eagerly.

'That's really sweet of you, Abha. I'll definitely come. What time, and who all are coming?' I asked, pleased with the fact that I was gonna spend one whole evening without thinking about Jay and Shanaya!

'Um it's you, me, Tejaswini, Pranita, Tanmay, Vihaan, and Durvesh. We'll meet at city ride at around six. Okay with you?' she asked, her voice booming with excitement about the plan.

'Count me in! I am on it!' I said, trying to match her level of enthusiasm.

'Cool then. Will meet ya tomorrow, will be fun. Bye. Take care,' she said, her voice sounding a bit dreamy, which made me laugh. Cute.

'Yeah, yeah, I'll be there. You too take care,' I said, ending the conversation.

I was really looking forward to the outing as due to all this Jay scenario, I really didn't mix up like before because all my attention was always towards 'What is Jay doing?' or 'Who is Jay with now?'

I paid special attention to my appearance that evening. I took more time than I usually take to select my dress, and at the end, I chose an aqua-blue one-piece which was an inch above my knees. It went well with my figure and enhanced my curves. I matched it with black studs in my ears and a silver Korean bracelet, metallic black heels, and a black clutch. I made up my hair differently than the normal one, where I keep them loose as it is. I tied it up in a bun and left strands of my hair out, letting them come up till my neck. I looked in the mirror, and satisfied with my appearance, I got ready to leave.

Going in the hall, I said, 'Mom, I am going out for that movie thing I told you yesterday. I may come home late, so don't wait for me.'

Mom came out and raised an eyebrow after having a proper look at my appearance. 'You are looking extremely beautiful! If only your dad would be here to see how you have grown up, he would be so proud of you!' she said, almost on the verge of breaking down. But in a matter of seconds, she regained her composure.

Dad was a really nerve-touching topic for me. I go in my silent mode; I retreat in my cave because I become vulnerable, way more than necessary. I became rigid, as rigid as a stone, after Mom's words.

Sensing what's happening to me, Mom started stroking my back and said, 'You are going to watch which movie anyways?' Her voice was as gentle, soft, and comforting as it could be!

I straightened myself, and urging myself to be stronger, I answered, 'Some Ranbir Kapoor movie, I guess. I am not in touch with Bollywood, Mom'

'Okay, okay, whatever. I'll ask the driver to drop you, and he will bring you back as well,' she said sternly and went out to call the driver.

Mom was trying her best to hide her emotions in front of me, but I could see through her facade. She was just trying to be strong for me so that I won't break down and I will have the strength to keep going on.

Life had taught me things in a very cruel way. In four words, I can sum up almost anything and everything I have learned about life: 'It simply moves on.' And you should move on too, or else you will be left nowhere. But there are some people who always seem to be in your heart, if not constantly on your mind, because out of sight is not necessarily out of mind.

The driver dropped me at the theatre, and they all were waiting for me outside.

'Hey, guys! Am I on time' I asked, breaking the ice.

'Yes, you are. Don't worry, even we arrived just like a minute ago,' Vihaan said, assuring me.

'You are looking very beautiful, mademoiselle!' Durvesh said, grinning and giving me a typical French bow.

I was glad I gelled in easily, and there was no discomfort, and Durvesh, being his usual charming self, made everyone comfortable.

'Ha ha! Thank you so much, monsieur.' I grinned back, and everyone started laughing.

Laughing and giggling, we went inside. It was the perfect start to my evening. I was at the popcorn stand, and boom, I banged into someone.

I was pissed at that person and hence I yelled at him. 'Are you blind? Can't you watch your step?' I said, busy straightening my dress.

'Who is gonna watch their step when you are in front,' he said with a mocking tone.

Shocked and taken aback, I looked up and no one will take a dime to guess who the person was!

'What are you doing here?' I asked Jay. Silly question, I know, but I couldn't think of anything else. One part of me was annoyed seeing him there, but one part of me was more than happy seeing him there.

'Why do people come to theatres, Aisha?' he asked, pulling my leg. 'Sigh, sigh . . . Am I affecting you so much that Miss Know-It–All is asking such questions?' He tried to suppress a smile.

'Don't you flatter yourself so much now, Jay!' I said, giving him a no-nonsense look.

'Ouch, that hurt my ego, ma'am. You hurt me,' he said, mocking his tears. 'By the way, you are looking at your quintessential best today!'

'Thanks, but I suppose you are in here with your fake beauty, so you enjoy with her, I'm off. Bye,' I said curtly, not waiting for his reply and going back to my group.

Tejaswini heard what happened, I guess, and she was looking at me with concern. After everyone was engrossed in something or other, she took me aside.

'You love Jay even now, don't you?' she asked rhetorically. 'You remember even back then, I used to tell you, but you never seemed to be in accordance with me.'

Tejaswini and I used to be pretty close back then. Like, after Jay, if there could be one friend who actually, truly knew me, it was her.

'Yes, genius, you were always right,' I said, revealing the innermost feelings on my face. It felt so good to tell this to someone. I felt like 100 kilos of weight had been lifted off my shoulders.

'Don't worry yourself out, gal, I think he reciprocates your feelings. I have observed him a lot. His attention is more towards you than towards Shanaya, and Shanaya has always forced herself upon him. So I doubt if he ever had any feelings for her in the first place,' she said, consoling me.

Those words did the trick, and day by day, things and situations were giving me hope that Jay loved me just as I loved him. Maybe he was just afraid of the consequences or something like that. Is that what he meant the other day when he left that sentence incomplete? Maybe he just needs a confirmation of my feelings! I suddenly entered 'bliss mode', and I swear to God, I loved my brain for deciphering this out! But I wasn't sure, and I am sure as hell not taking the first step, but just the fact that maybe Jay loves me brought back the spark in my eyes and inserted life in me.

'Thanks a ton, I surely needed it.' I smiled at her. I loved her and her benevolent nature.

We went to screen number 3 and took our seats. Jay was just one row behind me and was sitting diagonal to me, and on most part of that evening, I could see Jay's eyes on me. I was stealing a look or so as well when his attention was elsewhere.

That evening was awesome, and the bond between me and Tejaswini was kinda renewed and went back to its original best. I went home after a sorta memorable evening. Lying on the bed, I was thinking of all the memories of me and her—the secrets we shared, the distribution of projects between us, the way we always had each other's back. And also I was thinking about me and Jay—the time we spent solving each other's problems, knowing exactly what the other one had to say without conveying it through words, chatting nights and nights together, those surprises on our birthdays! Ah, those good old days.

I and Jay, we have a really out-of-this-world relationship! We fight today, then hug and smile and make up later. We argue tomorrow, but high-five soon. We have had our share of ups and downs and suns and moons. We have gone through a lot of things together, and we go through a lot daily as well, but at the end of the day, we are always together. Together always and forever because some relationships never die no matter what as their hearts are sewn by their souls.

Chapter 2

It had been a month since I was back in India, and I had to start looking out for a job soon. I had started looking out for those job ads in the newspapers, but there were a very few which actually interested me, and it was high time I started earning now. After all, for how many more days can I let Mom work! I didn't quite like the fact that she had to work, but given the situation, I had no choice, and neither did she. I was at the table that day, sipping my coffee while reading the newspaper.

'Jay's dad had called when you were asleep, he was asking for you,' Mom said, arbitrarily picking up the spoons.

'Huh? Did he leave any message?' I asked, dazed. Why would Uncle call me? I was amazed. Both father and son have the habit of flabbergasting me. As they say, like father, like son.

'Yeah, he has invited you over for dinner tonight. He said he wanted to thrash out about something important!' Mom said, keeping her countenance straight as if trying to conceal something. She was sure as hell behaving weird today, my mom; I don't know what's gotten into her.

Jay's dad was a highbrow, a man of superb taste—rich, natty, and preponderant. I had met him many times before but just for short periods as he was always busy in his office work.

'You are going right?' Mom asked.

'Um, I have to, don't I? I mean, I don't have any other alternative. I just wish I had an idea of what he is going to discuss,' I said, trying to reason out the invitation, but I was up to no avail.

'Stop saying like you are forced to go there! Jay is your best friend, and his dad has invited you over for dinner. Obviously, it must be for something good!' she said, and she was so sure of the fact it will be good.

'Mmm hmm . . . I am going, Mom so just relax,' I said, reassuring and soothing Mom and her flared up mind.

I was still confused why his dad had called me, and I swear I have no clue or even a faint hint or idea as to why I was summoned for dinner at the Singhania residence.

I was expected over there by 7 p.m., and at 6.30 p.m. sharp, I was ready to go to their place—nervous, anxious, confused, and slightly afraid. I decided to sneak into some traditional wear; maybe his parents will like me more! Anyways, tense I reached his place and rang the doorbell. It was Jay who opened the door.

'Whoa! Someone's looking lovely, and someone is in traditional wear! Now that's interesting,' he said, amused, going into his own thoughts.

I went inside, and with the most polite and revered smile, I greeted them by touching their feet. I have no clue as to why I did it, and I swear to God, I could see Jay trying to curb his smile. Auntie, Uncle, I, and Jay started talking while the servants served us dinner around 8.30 p.m. Jay even had a brother who was in Kolkata, marketing his second book. He is an author. He was two years older than us, I guess. I really don't know. I hardly have seen him.

'So tell me, have you found any interesting job offers yet, Aisha?' Uncle asked me, clearly interested in this topic. Men are always interested in business and job and money! Are all the other topics in the world dead?

Taking a deep breath, I answered, 'Not really . . . I mean I did check out some ads and stuff, but unfortunately, there was nothing which caught my eye.'

'Say fortunately nothing interested you much!' he said, his face beaming and earnest enthusiasm reflecting from his eyes.

'Excuse me? I didn't get you over here, Uncle!' I said, somewhat offended and completely confused. As I said before, both father and son have the habit of flabbergasting me.

'Explain it to her, Jay,' Uncle said, still smiling broadly.

If I stay here for one minute more, I swear I'll either go crazy or will end up saying or doing something inappropriate. I was looking at Jay intently, waiting for him to say something.

'Ash, Dad here wants you to join our company and work for us,' he said, and every word he said had so much energy and gusto that it would surely light up a 100-watt bulb!

'Not only do I want that, I also want you and Jay to work together on every project given to both of you,' his dad said. His tone was insistent and demanding, and his voice had that typical superior type tone to it. It was as if he had ordered that to me.

'Uncle, I will love to work for you, but I don't want you to give me this job just because I and Jay are close friends. Give me a post which is permitted inside my qualifications. If you think I am qualified to do the job you are offering me, I'll be ready to join any time you ask me,' I said calmly and very maturely, maintaining my composure.

'What? Aisha, are you mad or—' Jay was saying, but his dad interrupted him.

'Wait, son, let me talk to her,' he told Jay, and giving him that 'don't you interrupt me now' look, he said, 'Look, Aisha, I am not offering you this post or job because you are related to Jay in any way. I am a businessman, and when it comes to business, I am very practical and pardon no relationships, so I am warning you, working with me will be tough and as far as your qualifications are concerned, you are perfect for this post. I hope we are clear on this now.' He was content and pleased with his answer.

Mighty my, I was silent after Uncle's short speech. I was very carefully thinking of what to say but came up with a really lame reply after five whole minutes of silence.

'Thank you, Uncle, for thinking I am ideal for this post. It means a lot. It will be a pleasure and an honour working with you,' I said confidently as if I were as intelligent as Einstein or Hawking.

Uncle gave me that typical sweet parental type of smile. The way he and his smile transformed when we talked about business and now that it was all done was miraculous. Trust me, I was all impressed. I wonder how he manages two different sides of his at the same time, and the big question I have is that which one is the real one?

While I was thinking about my new job, Jay elbowed me, and adding a sugar-sweet coat to his tone, he said, 'Welcome to the company, Ash, and don't say thanks because the pleasure is totally all mine.' He winked at me and gave me his notorious dimpled smile.

Gosh! I was a sucker for that smile of his. That smile melted me completely, and all the insecurity, uncertainty, and anger which had evolved in me since the day he introduced me to *his* Shanaya just vanished in a matter of seconds, and I again became the same Aisha who had fallen head over heels for her best friend six darn years ago!

The rest of the evening went by swiftly, and I was supposed to start working with him next week. The job security and Uncle's confidence in me gave an impulsive, natural, and much-needed boost to my self-confidence, and Jay's behaviour towards me gave birth to hope again and gave a different angle to my life. I had started enjoying and loving my life again. Before coming back to India, I had dreaded to even imagine how my life will be when I would be back in India.

Sometimes I wonder, how can one person, just one person, matter so much that you give them an immense power—a power which gives their words and actions the strength to determine your happiness and sorrow, that what they say to you can either break you or make you? And our brain is never even close to deciphering the reasons our heart has which made that stupid red thing fall so badly in love. Our heart is sure as hell a very sly thing! Never let's our brain know anything!

I was so profoundly engrossed in my own thoughts that I didn't realize that Jay was saying something! He had to shake me literally, and then I realized that he was saying something.

'Dream gal comes out of her dreams! Finally! Aisha, I was talking to you for the past five minutes, and all you were doing was looking at me dreamily and smiling, which was kinda cute, but coming back to the subject, what the heck were you thinking that got you so engrossed?' he asked me, and he was so bewildered and perplexed as he had never seen me like this, all dazed and dreamy.

For a split second, I had a huge urge to tell him that I was thinking about him and only he had the power to reduce my will to nil, but then my aptitude got the better of my feelings, and I answered, 'Nothing in particular. A lot of things, mostly about my years in Paris nothing else!'

His face became thoughtful, and there was a question mark on his face as if he had realized something. He felt his realization was pretty late, but then coming back to me, he asked, 'What is your relationship status? Do you still, er, love that guy, um, what was his name again? Chris, yeah, Chris!' he said every word in that sentence so carefully as if his life depended on it or he had bet some 500-odd million dollars and he was asking for the outcome.

I was a bit taken aback due to his tone and even frightened a bit, to be frank, but I feigned to find that question humorous, and faking a laugh, I said, 'Why does that bother you, Jay Singhania? But just for the record, I am not single, but nor am I committed. I'm simply on reserve only for that one person who deserves me and my heart, and as far as Chris is concerned, I do not love him, and I never loved—' My sentence was left incomplete because Auntie and Uncle came in to bid me a final adieu as they were retiring to bed.

I saw the time, and it was well past ten thirty! Darn, I didn't realize it had got so late. I called up Mom because I was sure she would be worried sick and up for me. I assured her I was okay and will reach home in half an hour or so!

'Can you drop me home? Our driver has gone home, and it's too late to catch an auto or taxi, and I really don't remember the roads, plus everything in here has changed,' I said in a very benignant tone, zonked.

'You don't need to ask that! Do you think I was going to let you go just like that so late at night? Like, seriously, Ash?' he asked, his tone sounding offended, and he was pissed, I guess.

'No no no! I was, er, just, um, you know, formality types, asking!' I said, not wanting a lecture from him.

He gave me one look, which made it quite clear to me that he knew I was lying to him. We silently went down. I don't quite like silence. It annoys me, but just now, it was doing nothing except scaring the hell out of me.

In the parking lot, he suddenly held my arms tight, and shaking my entire frame, he asked me, 'Don't you trust me any more, Aisha? Do I mean anything to you now or . . . ?' His voice was breaking at the end. He could not complete the sentence, and he just moved away from me.

I was shocked and even stunned seeing him in this state. I had never ever in my entire life seen Jay like this, so vulnerable and fragile. It was like he would fall like a pack of cards any moment. It hurt me seeing him in this condition, and knowing that I was the cause of all of it didn't really help.

'Jay, you are one person I trust the most in the world. You and my mom are the most significant and important people in my life. Are we clear on this topic now?' I asked, looking at him deeply and intensely.

I so wanted to say many more things, but that would surely bring to light each and every ounce and bit of my

27

feelings towards him, so I just decided to hush myself as that was the best thing I could do, or else the cat would be out of the bag!

'So long, so good,' he murmured, and we got into the car.

The whole ride, we both were silent. None of us said a word. Those stares were shared equally in between during the drive. He dropped me home, and while he was leaving he said, 'If it helps or makes you feel better, then know one thing—you are the most important person in my world, and you matter to me more than anyone else.' That look on his face convinced me that he meant every word he spoke and no one could question the authenticity in his eyes!

I gave him a warm, genuine, and love-filled smile, and I guess everything I wanted to say was conveyed through that smile, and winking back, he drove off. Small gestures say a lot more than they should.

I went inside, reassured Mom I am safe and went straight to my room. Those words had started taking a toll on me, and I was starting to lose my composure, and incontestably, I didn't wanna do that in front of Mom, and I preferred the tranquillity that my room offered.

I was rolling on my bed from one side to the other. So much was said today. Not many words were exchanged between me and him, but a lot was conveyed through trifle things. It is always the small things which matter. After all, great things are made up by bringing together a series of small things. It's always the small things which give us happiness. The happiness you get when the person you love with all your heart and soul says 'I love you' cannot be matched by a pay cheque or you getting a promotion. Or the satisfaction you get when your parents have a smile on their faces because of you can nowhere be compared to you owning a multimillion house or many luxurious SUVs. And what Jay said today made me feel as if I were the most special person in the world. I was on cloud nine. My emotions had reached their zenith, and my happiness knew no bounds. This was no doubt one of the most memorable nights of my existence; it would definitely make it to the top 5! Listening to Basshunter's 'All I Ever Wanted', I merrily glided into a deep and serene sleep.

The whole of the next week went into shopping for my clothes as I had to start my job on Monday, parties, going out with friends, and chit-chats and gossip with Mom, and the bonus was that I met an old friend from school, Shwetha. It felt nice meeting her after eons, and it even made me realize how much I have changed.

There was a party at Shanaya's place on Saturday, and I was surprised like anything to receive an invitation. Karishma, I, and Tejaswini were going together as all three of us despised that rich, spoiled brat. Abha and Pranita were gonna come together, I suppose, as they lived nearby but at the other end of the city.

We reached the party a bit late, and by the time we arrived, the party was on in full swing. Shanaya was entertaining the guests, and for a change, she was not arm in arm and hand in hand with Jay. In fact, Jay was nowhere around her. He was in one corner, and he looked a bit drunk from the confounded and dazed look on his face.

'Just look at the way she is gushing about her shenanigans. "When I went to Europe I did this, when I went to America

I did that"!' Karishma said, imitating Shanaya, and all three of us started laughing.

Karishma was a joyous person to be around with. You can never be gloomy or sad when you're with her! She has an uncanny gift of predicting the stocks as well as making you laugh. She can make you laugh anywhere and everywhere, and the cherry on the cake was that she was a really hot and good-looking chick—a perfect catch for any guy, I would say.

Suddenly, there were loud noises coming from the sitting room, and all of us rushed in.

'I don't love you, Shanaya! I don't!' Jay yelled at her.

Those words definitely brought a smile on my face but brought tears to that gal's eyes. I somehow felt awful for her, and I could really understand how she was feeling at that moment.

Shanaya was very rich, spoiled, and pampered. She was always used to getting what she wanted and also used to people wanting to be like her or be with her. Unquestionably, it must have been a big, huge blow for her, and those words must have hit her pretty hard, I guess.

'Jay, why are you doing this to me? We were going so good and strong. Where did I go wrong?' she asked, her voice literally begging and pleading. The pain could be guessed, and I felt really horrible now.

Jay was drunk, and hence his words were too harsh. To handle the situation somehow and also because I could no longer endure the pain Shanaya was going through, I intervened.

'Shanaya, I think rest upon it now, Jay is drunk! He is not in his senses, and hence all the gibberish talks just now.

I think it's best if he goes home now and takes rest. He needs it, and so do you,' I said, genuinely concerned and worried about both of them.

'You don't teach me what to do, and you sure as hell don't get to decide when and where my boyfriend goes!' she yelled, taking out all the anger and frustration on me.

'Take it easy, Shanaya. Listen to me once, and then do whatever you want,' I said firmly yet gently.

Everyone came along and helped Shanaya calm her nerves. I informed Tejaswini and Karishma that I am taking Jay and going home, and they both came with me as well. I called up Jay's mom and informed her that Jay met with a small accident and he has hurt his calf a bit so he would be resting at my place.

'Thanks for the help, both of you. I will let you know what happened tomorrow morning. Take care and get home safe,' I whispered to both of them and waved them goodbye.

Mom had slept long back as I had already informed her that I would be coming in late. Jay was really drunk, and he was saying really silly and lame things.

'You know you are beautiful, right?' he said, pulling my cheeks and laughing. I swear he was acting crazy!

'Let me put you in the guest's bedroom, then I'll give you some medicine,' I said, heaving out a sigh.

'You are the best, Ash! Way to go! Wohoooo!' He was screaming now, making me blush.

I took him to the spare room and made him lie down. I gave him a tablet and ordered him to have it.

'Is there anything else I can get you? Do you need anything else?' I asked modestly, and I was way too tired too.

'You! All I want is you. You'll drive all the harm away. Just say you are mine,' he said, and he was high, very high.

'We'll talk tomorrow when you're sober,' I said, afraid that I may pass out any moment.

He walked up to me, stumbling in his steps. He just looked at me. I stared back. Whenever I look at his face, trust me, every single time, I forget to breathe. I get dazed, and every single time I see him, I get shocked as to how someone can be so strikingly good-looking. It was a face anyone in the world would trade their life for—the perfect curve of his lips, those fine arches of his cheekbones, that perfect jawline he has, and his eyes. I save his eyes till the end because I know that every time I look in those grey eyes of his, I lose track of everything, even my thoughts!

Taking advantage of my blankness at the moment, he came forward. He came close to me, very close, and he kissed me, and without realizing what I was doing, I kissed him back, like an idiot! Knowing what the consequences could be, knowing that he had a bloody girlfriend for crying out loud, I still kissed him back.

Pulling myself back, I said with tears in my eyes, 'You ass! Go to sleep!' And I stormed out of the room in tears.

I should have hated him after all this, but no, I didn't! They righteously say, 'Love is blind, and it knows no boundaries.' How can love overpower you so much? Love is the perfection found in every flaw. It's blind yet it spots trifle goodness in every moment. It is felt in every pulse, and it beats in every heart, even in my heart, and my heart just beats for Jay, and that's all I know and care for.

The next day, he slept till noon, and by then, I cooked up a story and fed Mom. By the time he got up, Mom had already gone out. I saw him come out of the room but paid no attention.

'Is it too much to ask for a cup of coffee?' he asked innocently and modestly.

'Sure.' I said and went inside the kitchen to make some coffee, but he followed me inside.

'Are you still furious with me because of what happened last night?' he asked, and he seemed a bit dizzy.

'Yes, I am! You have a girlfriend whose name is Shanaya and yet you kissed me! I am sorry, but I am not that type of a gal who does all this,' I shrieked at him, my voice emotional.

'Is that what you thought when I kissed you? That I wanna keep Shanaya but be with you as well?' he asked, shocked and enraged.

'Obviously! Any decent gal on this damned earth would think so!' I bellowed back.

'Wasn't it very clear from yesterday's incident that I do not love Shanaya?' he moaned. 'I am not gonna even look at you until I get this straight!' His words were as sharp as the tip of a sword, and saying so, he stormed out of my house.

I just stood there in silence. My head was aching badly. I felt weak, very weak. I felt as if I will faint the next minute, my knees going wobbly. I dumped myself on the chair beside me when Mom came in.

'Where's Jay? And what's with you? You seem as if you will fall down next minute. You are a mess, sweetheart. Let's get you to the room, and I will put you to sleep,' Mom said softly.

She took me to my room, gave me a painkiller, and put me to sleep. The drugs in the tablet made me slip into a deep sleep in a few minutes. I woke up in the evening, my condition no better than what it was at noon. I checked my phone to see if Jay had called or texted, but except from Jay, I had received messages from almost all my friends. I was on the verge of losing my mind. I couldn't think of anything but Jay. I wanted to weep and lament, but I kept myself steady and went down. Mom very well knew that something had gone wrong between me and Jay, and from her expressions, it looked as if she had worried herself out over me.

She saw me coming down, and it was as if she had been waiting for me to come down. 'Are you better now, Aisha?' she asked me in a placid and soft tone, and it was very obvious that my condition bothered her like anything.

'I am good, Mom. Don't worry too much. It is okay, Mom I am okay, and I mean it,' I said, trying to assure her that all was fine, but it was of no use. She knew I wasn't one bit all right.

Trying to divert my attention from whatever was bothering me, Mom said, 'So are you ready for tomorrow?'

'What's new tomorrow, Mom' I asked shakily, my head paining. I felt like my head was into splits.

'Aisha, are you in your senses? How could you forget what's tomorrow?' she asked, shocked and a bit infuriated and displeased.

And then it struck me that it was Monday tomorrow! Oh freaking shit! I am supposed to start working tomorrow, and whether fortunately or unfortunately, I seriously don't know; I had to start working with Jay tomorrow. I really don't know what is gonna happen tomorrow, and I don't even wanna think about how appallingly ghastly my day is gonna be tomorrow. I can literally imagine those unkind stares, the uncomfortable exchanges of words, the taunts which I am going to receive from Jay from tomorrow onwards. Maybe I should just tell Uncle I can't work with him, but that would be too rude, and I can't be that type of a gal who conveys ungratefulness.

'Oh yeah, Mom, I remember. Don't fuss about it, Mom, and I am in no mood or state to argue over this topic just now. So please drop it,' I said, and Mom was not looking really pleased with the fact that I was not giving much importance to tomorrow.

'Fine, but just know one thing, it's a new chapter in your life, and unquestionably, you will face difficulties, but you have to overcome those hurdles and move ahead. Now enough with the heavy things, let's have a light dinner,' Mom said, trying to joke around and uplift my mood.

'Oh nice, Mom, I like it!' I exclaimed, trying to ease off the pressure on her.

I tried to behave as normal as possible in front of Mom so she would think that now I am really better. I can do anything for my mom. Trust me, I love her insanely. I miss Dad too, and that to a lot, but then I find the same security and protectiveness when I am with Jay, and hence my love for him is ten times the normal love.

I went to sleep beside Mom today. I don't know why, but I felt safe sleeping beside her as if she was guarding me from everything which could hurt me and as if she was my safe and protective harbour. I slept dreaming of things I desired and wanted from the innermost nerve and vein of my heart. They say some of the greatest things in life are unseen; that's why we always close our eyes when we kiss, dream, or cry.

The next morning, for the first time since I had come to India, I woke up as early as 6 a.m. I went for a jog, trying to remove disturbing thoughts, and it really worked. I love running. It gives me a sense of freedom, and it gives me an opportunity to explore different things in me as well as in nature.

By 9.30 a.m., I was ready to leave, and I had reached the office at ten sharp. I liked reaching places on time. Punctuality was something I admired, and Jay was never ever punctual. Jay didn't show up till 11 a.m., and I had finished discussing all the details about my studies and qualifications with Uncle—I mean Jay's dad—when Prince Charming arrived.

'From tomorrow onwards, if you do not reach office at the same time as every other staff out there reaches, you won't find a place in here,' Uncle told him. His tone was calm, yet there was firmness and sternness in there. I myself was terrified by Uncle's words, and that gave a hint to how he actually didn't pardon relationships when it came to business.

'Okay, Dad, sorry' was all Jay could say, and he himself was taken aback.

Uncle left us with huge files for us to know about the history and, over all, everything about the company. He gave us just fifteen days to go through all those dreadful, huge, and mind-numbing files, reports, and statistics.

I quietly picked up one file and started reading.

'Damn you, Aisha! Won't you even ask me why I came late?' he asked, his lips ending into a straight grimace.

I gave him a hard look, and sighing, I asked him, 'Why were you late, Jay?'

Gulping in air, taking a deep breath as if he were a slave who was freed from the shackles of slavery, he said in a pleased and benevolent tone, 'I. Broke up. With. Shanaya.' He paused after every word so that each word gets equal importance.

My eyes widened with surprise, and I swear my eyeballs were on the brink of popping out like table tennis balls! I still couldn't believe what I just heard.

'Why would you do that?' I asked, dreamily and vaguely distracted.

'You have to come with me to Vihaan's place for sometime after office ends. Over there, you'll get the answers to all your questions. Till then keep some persistence.'

'Why should I come?' I asked, not really interested in meeting or bumping into Shanaya.

'You'll come because I say so,' he answered back and gave me a long, firm look which clearly hinted danger, so I decided neither to argue with him nor to press the topic any further.

Time flew by in a spur, and before I knew, it was time to go. Without any questions, I sat into the front seat of his Audi Q5, and we drove off. We reached Vihaan's place, and each and every friend (except Shanaya of course) we had was present there to witness something I had no clue of.

'Speak up, buddy, now is the time,' Vihaan said, quietly patting Jay's back.

Okay, so Vihaan knew what it was, but I didn't. Surprising yet interesting. Suddenly, Jay gestured something, and everyone started coming closer, forming a circle around us, and before I realized what was happening, Jay held my hand and went down on one knee.

'Aisha Mukherjee, I love you, and I always loved you right since the first time I saw you in ninth grade. It was love at first sight, and I instantly fell for your simplicity, your brains, the overly caring nature you have, your benignancy and benevolence, and not to mention those pretty features and that cute, childlike smile. Ah! I still soften up and liquefy at the sight of that smile. I love every freaking single thing about you, even the anger and haughtiness you display at times. I am irreversibly and frantically in love with you, and I promise to love you every single day of forever,' he said with intense and fanatical love dripping from each and every word of his, and sincerity rang in his eyes.

I was too overwhelmed and ecstatic to say anything, but my eyes were moist, and I realized that I was crying. People were looking at me, waiting for me to say something.

'I love you too, Jay, with all my heart and soul, and you were the sole one to have ever captured my heart and soul,' I said, and we hugged each other.

I was so happy, blissful. It was like a dream come true for me. I got the guy I loved truly and dearly since eons— finally! I was so content and satisfied being there in his arms that I didn't wanna leave him. People had started their coughing to pull our legs, and I blushed, my cheeks as red as a tomato.

Tejaswini was the first one to come and give me the congratulatory hug, and winking at me, she whispered in my ears, 'I was right all the way,' and chuckled.

Karishma, Abha, Vihaan, Durvesh, Pranita, Tanmay, et al.—everyone came in, hugged me and Jay, and gave the usual compliments. Even Kruttika did, and I was surprised. As she was Shanaya's best friend, I would have never expected her to be here. But Kruttika right from the very beginning was always known as a person with a big heart, so I shouldn't be that surprised, I guess. She is pretty sweet.

He took me to the car to drop me home, and I just kept gaping and gawking at him. He chuckled and said, 'Look at you, Ash!' Then sighing he said, 'How did I get so lucky?' asking the question more to himself than to me.

'Shh!' I silenced him, and standing up on my toes, I kissed him passionately with all my will and power. 'I love you beyond limits and boundaries. If you ever leave me, there will be no Aisha Mukherjee in the world thereafter,' I said, giving out smalls sobs.

'Hey, sweetheart, easy please . . . I will never ever leave you, and if I ever do, I am darn sure it will be my last breath,' he said, gazing into my eyes with love, compassion, adoration, and generosity.

He dropped me home, hummed an 'I love you', and went home.

I went inside with my face beaming, and there was a new glow on my face. It was as if I had just climbed the Mount Everest!

'Looks like someone had a remarkable day,' Mom said, nudging me in the stomach.

'I, er, need to tell you something, Mom' I said it quite uneasily, and it was the first time I was afraid over the reaction my mom would give over the words I say and the news she hears.

'Yes, go on . . . I am all yours and ears!' she said, laughing over the sentence, but sensing my discomfort, she knew there was something important to be told.

'Mom, er, I and Jay . . . Um, we're, uh, together!' I said, cautiously choosing every word with utmost care.

'That was bound to happen sooner or later, and I had expected it even earlier, but as they say, better late than never!' she said, and she really didn't react to anything like what I had expected her to!

Astounded and surprised, I asked her, 'Aren't you angry?'

'Give me one good reason to get angry. In fact, I am really happy that you both are finally together and my daughter finally got her long-time crush, and he is the perfect match for you,' she said, still engrossed more in cutting the cauliflower properly.

I just told Mom I am in a relationship, and this is the reaction I get—something completely paradoxical to what I had imagined. 'Long-time crush? You knew it right from the beginning?' I asked, bowled over.

'It's not that hard to guess, sweetie. You're an open book for me, and once upon a time, even I was your age,' she said, smiling at me, kissing my forehead.

'I am going to my room. I already am done with dinner, and I assume you are done too?' I asked with a raised eyebrow in her direction.

'Yes, yes . . . I am done. Now go hop to your room and let the day sink in. Enjoy.' She winked and forced me to take some almond shake with me just in case I get hungry.

As soon as I was in the serenity of my room, the thought process started. All the happenings of the day were finally starting to penetrate, and I was trying to convince myself that all this was not just one more dream of mine but it was the reality which came true after years and years of waiting and patience. Ah! How much I love, Jay. There's no one else in the entire world who can love him as much as I do. There's nothing in the world which can be compared to my love for him, nothing. I love him so very much. He matters the world to me, and no one can ever replace him in my life, no one can. We never went to candlelit dinners and dates and stuff. Real love is not based upon romance, candlelit dinners, walks along the beach, etc. In fact, it's based on care, compromise, respect, and trust.

Love is larger than life and twice as natural. Love is when somebody becomes the centre of your world, the centre of your universe, and eventually the centre of you. It is when somebody affects you the most, inspires you the most, runs in your mind 24/7, and jogs in front of your eyes all day. It is when that person's happiness means the world to you and that person becomes an extension of you and re-devises you in a better way, develops you as a person, and evolves you and within you. It is when you can, without thinking, say anything to that person and still be sure he won't judge you, someone whose companionship means everything to you and you can't really live without that person. It's rare for all these qualities to come together, but when they do come together, it is definitely *real love*.

Chapter 3

I couldn't sleep last night, hence I seemed quite exhausted and tired. I couldn't sleep because reality was far better and far more beautiful than my dreams could be. One of the signs of being in love is not being able to sleep, and Mom found my appearance hilarious somehow and was not able to control her amusement; her mirth was shaking the whole dining table!

'Are you done now, Mom?' I asked, pleased seeing her smile wholeheartedly after eons altogether.

'Yeah, yeah, I am finally done! Oh gosh! You should have seen yourself walk down the stairs. Ruffled hair all spread out, eyes puffed due to lack of sleep, tired and exhausted, and still grinning!' Mom said, trying to control her laughter now.

After hearing all this and seeing Mom laugh again, even I couldn't help smiling.

'Mom, I am really glad I amuse you, but now I really need to get ready for office, and I can't be late or Hitler uncle will get mad,' I said, pressing the ends of my head.

'That's not the way you convey you gratitude, Aisha!' she scolded me. 'You get ready, till then I'll prepare your breakfast.'

'Okay, okay, fine,' I said, retreating, and then kissing her forehead, I left to get ready.

I was ready by nine thirty, and as I was about to leave, there was a loud honking of a car. The horn was a very familiar one, and I went outside, blushing and smiling. He was leaning by his Audi Q5, dressed in formals with black glares which perfectly went with his oval face, and I felt like he was a hot model standing for a freaking international magazine's photo shoot!

'I see that someone likes the way I am looking today!' he said, smiling my favourite dimpled smile.

His smile lit up my world like those thousand little diyas illuminating the whole country during Diwali, and I felt like singing, 'Baby, you light up my world like nobody else.' His smile ended the gloom and darkness just like the sun eradicates the darkness of the night by marking its presence.

'I see someone is on time today after what happened yesterday!' I said, grinning back and also getting back at him.

We reached the office at the given time, and I bet everyone could notice the difference. There was something there. The new chemistry between us, the glow and happiness on our faces, the love and care for each other in our eyes, the aura around us, and the constant stares and holding of hands were not something people didn't notice.

We were working on a file when his dad entered.

'This is not something I will tolerate. Both of you learn to behave yourselves. This is my office, and I want no nonsense here,' he said, his words very harsh and sharp but his pitch as soft as if he was talking to a toddler.

I have no words to tell how embarrassed I was in front of Jay's dad. There had to be something to spoil my day, or else how could my day be complete! I was as red as an apple, and I was ashamed of my behaviour, downright ashamed. How could I lose my senses and behave like this at my workplace? I was behaving like a fourteen-year-old teenager who had fallen in love for the first time. The only difference was that a teen is controlled by his/her hormones and I was being controlled by my heart.

'We are very sorry, sir. It is now that I realize how stupid and childish we were behaving. It won't be repeated ever again. I promise you that this won't happen again. One more thing, sir, we were going through the Urja project's details, and there is something we'd like to discuss about it with you. That is when you are free, sir,' I said in the humblest way possible and with firmness and confidence in my voice, not letting it falter or break in any way.

After I told Uncle I wanted to talk about the Urja project, his expressions changed on the whole. I knew Urja was his favourite and his dearest project, and it was a project he was very proud of. He looked mighty pleased and flattered that I chose Urja of all the projects to look into first. Aha . . . Nice, so buttering works on my soon-to-be father-in-law. Good for me; I am pretty good with buttering people up anyways.

'It's okay, you both are human after all, just make sure this never happens again, and as far as the project is concerned, come to my cabin in an hour or so,' he said, his tone sweet and words sugary.

'This goes for you as well, Jay, and it won't get any better if you don't concentrate on projects,' he said, a bit harsh.

'I understand . . .' he started.

I sensed he didn't have anything to say, and hence interrupting him, I said, 'Sir, it was actually his idea to look into the Urja project.'

He smiled and nodded sideways, and his smile somehow reminded me of my dad when something was very apparent to him.

'Ash, Dad can make out when you lie, and not only Dad, everyone can! You suck at lying!' he chuckled and hugged me, kissing my hair.

We went to Uncle's cabin and discussed even the minutest details of his much-preferred project. Pleased with our discussions, he gave us the rest of the evening free.

'I need to show you something. Come with me,' he said, holding my waist.

'What is it?' I asked a bit curious.

'It's something really close to my heart and a place I always visit when I am upset or down, but anyhow, I make it a point to visit it at least once a week,' he said, and I could see that this place was really close to his heart as he spoke about it with a lot of adoration.

'Super! I'm all excited and keyed up!' I said, my tone revealing clearly my keenness and enthusiasm of going to the place Jay loved so much.

We left, and he took me to an area which was really not that familiar to me.

'Where are we exactly?' I asked, a bit puzzled and confused.

'Do you remember Mom and Dad had gifted me a small one -BHK- apartment on my seventeenth birthday?' he asked.

'Um, yeah, I do remember,' I said. When he had told me about the gift, I was so taken aback. I mean who gifts one whole freaking apartment on a birthday! *Rich people and their rich gifts*, I thought and sighed.

'That's where we are going,' he said, his tone trying to conceal his excitement.

He stopped the car outside that apartment of his. We went inside the lift, and he pressed the button with number 6 on it. The lift stopped on the sixth floor, and we were standing outside his apartment.

'I need to tie a cloth around your eyes.' Barely could he speak properly. He was literally shivering with excitement.

'But why?' I was protesting, but then agreed, not wanting to spoil his excitement.

He tied a thick black cloth around my eyes and opened the lock. He guided me inside.

'Open your eyes now, Aisha,' he whispered in my ears and gave me a peck on my cheek.

I removed the cloth, and in front of me on all four sides of the wall were numerous pictures of mine, right from my ninth-grade braces and double ponytail look in school to my college look and even my recent pictures. I was dazed and benumbed and was at complete lack of words. He was standing there silently, carefully observing, analyzing and taking in each and every reaction and expression on my face.

'I love this place. It's very dear to me. This place gives me hope, you give me hope. It lightens my mood,' he said, coming from behind and holding me in his arms.

I still was in a state of numbness and in shock. He even had some of my childhood pictures and pictures which were clicked in France, and I had no idea how he got them! A room full of my pictures! This is berserk! This guy standing next to me is berserk! I mean this is total craziness! Who does all this! But I loved what I saw, and I love him for this, and this even showed how much he loves me.

'When did you put all the pictures? This month or the last month or when?' I asked.

'Ash, all these pictures were with me since the time I saw you, and all this I have been putting on the walls since I got this apartment,' he said, looking at me with extreme love and adoration in his eyes.

'I love you, more than you know!' I said and hugged him.

When I fell in love with him six to seven years back, that time I thought I had no scope with him, but I wanted him more than anything. I loved him more than anything, and he was the one I had given my heart and my soul to, but I knew I would never get him. It was so hard to wait for him as I knew he would never be mine, but it was even harder to give up when I knew he was everything I wanted. Now when I realize that he loved me too, maybe even more than I did, the feeling of satisfaction that he truly, actually loves me and that I am not one more notch in the belt for Mr Casanova was beyond explanation.

'Let's get going. I need to drop you home, and I think Auntie will start worrying now,' he said, and for one last time, he took me very close to him, and I could see through his eyes that he loved me dearly.

He dropped me home, and that was the end of one of the most beautiful and memorable days of my existence.

People you meet in the journey of life expect a lot of things from you, but there are some idiots who expect nothing more than just you, and he was one of those people who expected nothing from me except me and my love.

The next few days went in the same routine: Jay, office with Jay, Jay. So basically, we were together 24/7, and we did behave ourselves in the office and went out on dates, movies, to that apartment of his, etc. But due to him, it was like I had no time for my girlfriends, and by that, I mean my best friends who are gals. So I hatched up a plan.

'Hello, Tejaswini?' I asked. I had called her up.

'Did someone finally get time for me?' she said sarcastically, and she was clearly pissed.

'Ah, nothing like that re, it was due to office work!' I tried calming her down.

'You don't give me lame reasons now. I know very well who keeps you so obsessed and busy these days. Not that I blame him though,' she said, trying to tease me.

'Yeah, yeah . . . Anyways, your favourite hero's movie was released yesterday, and I have some passes, so I was wondering if you could come?' I asked her. We both knew I was pulling her leg, and we both were desperate to meet each other.

'Um, lemme think. I'll check out my schedule and see if I am free,' she said, chuckling.

Laughing, I said, 'I am counting you in. Let's meet at X-square tomorrow at, let's say, six, and I'll call the other three idiots too!' I said, giggling.

'All cool with me as long as you come!' she said in her *epic tone* she used when she wanted to taunt me.

'Ha ha! I'll be there. So meet ya tomorrow. Till then, take care, babe!' I said.

'Yeah, bye, and as far as take care goes, Jay does that exceedingly well.' She pulled my leg, and we ended the conversation.

I called up Karishma, Abha, and Pranita, and they all agreed.

The next day went the usual, with Jay coming to pick me up for the office, then the tedious files at the office with Jay, and his lame jokes for company. After office, he dropped me home and insisted that he drive me to the theatre. I changed, and he came to drop me.

Abha was the only one who had arrived.

'Hey! How long since you arrived?' I asked her, hoping I wasn't too late.

'Some five-odd minutes. I guess,' she said, winking towards me. 'Jay has come too. I see.' She grinned.

'Not in front of him, at least!' I said and blushed a deep scarlet.

'Don't you worry, Abha, I am not going to steal your best friend from you. I just came to drop her,' he said, trying to keep his smirk down.

Turning towards me, he said, 'Please get home before it gets too late, and if you stay beyond ten, then call me, I'll pick you up. Don't catch a cab so late.'

'Stop worrying so much. But if this makes you feel better, then fine, I'll do it,' I said, winking at him, and I pressed his hand softly.

We murmured a goodbye and hummed an 'I love you' to each other, and then he left. After a few minutes, the rest of them joined us, and we went in for the movie. I thoroughly enjoyed the evening, and it was all fun and amusing. I reached home by nine thirty and sent a message of the same to Jay. He called me up.

'You home, right?' he asked.

'I messaged you saying so, Jay!' I said, trying to keep myself awake. I was too tired and sleepy.

'Okay. You seem darn exhausted. Go and sleep,' he said very gently.

'Yeah, okay then, I'll meet you tomorrow. I am very sleepy. I love you,' I replied.

'I love you too. Goodnight and take care,' he said, ending our conversation.

Thinking about how fortunate I am to get a guy as sweet, loving, caring, and understanding like Jay and how very lucky I was to have awesome friends in my life and my dear sweet mom, I thanked God and tripped into a blissful sleep.

Every passing minute, every passing day, and every passing week, the bond between us kept on growing stronger, and our love became even stronger than before. When someone loves you more than their life, then that love gives you strength, and when you love someone more than your life, then that love gives you courage, they say. And here I was being loved by Jay more than his life, and I love him more than my life. He had transformed me into a stronger and more courageous Aisha, and like the phoenix, I rose from my own ashes.

It had been more than a month now that I and Jay were together. I was very happy these days and very busy. My mornings and evenings were occupied by Jay and sometimes my friends, and the middle of the day was occupied by office work. It was a Sunday, and I had cancelled all outings so as to spend some time with Mom. I had been seriously unfair towards her. I had given almost no time to her, and I felt guilty over it now, very guilty.

'Morning, Mom!' I exclaimed and hugged her.

'I see. Extra affection is being showered today, I wonder why! Do you want something?' she asked.

Now that certainly annoyed me, but then it's not her fault. I have hardly given her any time in the past two to three weeks. My mom and I only had each other to claim as our own. My mom had no siblings and neither did my dad, and both my grandparents were dead a long-time back.

'I don't want anything, Mom. I just missed you a lot these two to three weeks.' Then with a more serious tone, I said, 'Hey, Mom, even though sometimes I may not be able to give you all my time like before, that doesn't mean my love for you is lessening or something like that, you know? I love you a lot, Mom.' I tried to control the tears trying to come out of my eyes. Tears always ruin things!

This brought tears in Mom's eyes as well. We are very similar. We both are emotional, sensitive, short-tempered, etc.

'I love you too, Aisha, and you don't need to tell me that. I know that . . .' she said, holding my hand and winking.

'So how about today you rest the whole day, and I make you some breakfast!' I said, proposing the idea to her.

'Did I hear you right? Did you just say you will cook?' she exclaimed with excitement and astonishment as if what I said had taken the wind out of her.

'Yes, Mom, I said I'll make some breakfast for you,' I said with a scowl. I knew she would react like that. I have never, to date, cooked anything. I despise cooking; I have never stepped in the kitchen to make anything but coffee.

'The kitchen will be honoured today!' Mom said, laughing herself out.

I made breakfast, and we both ate it merrily, recounting our fights over her earnest desire to teach me how to cook. Time flies away, but the memories you have last forever.

We spent the whole day talking, laughing, gossiping, and then we went shopping and dined at Mom's favourite restaurant in the city. We had a memorable day, but the bottom line was she was very happy, and I was more than content seeing her happy! Her happiness means the world to me, especially since Dad's death I had to fill in his side as well as mine. I knew I wasn't doing too well, but I wanted Mom to know that I love her and will love her always and forever.

'Can I sleep in your room today with you?' I asked very innocently.

'Sweetheart, you are more than welcome,' she said, kissing my forehead.

It reminds me of my childhood and how I used to curl around Mom and sleep peacefully and how everything was so perfect back then.

The next day, I got up early and made Mom's favourite breakfast, i.e. French toast and spaghetti. I tidied everything and even cut some veggies for her and took some tea for her to the bedroom. Mom was getting royal treatment. How I crave for royal treatment! Then I went to the office, and the regular day passed.

A week had gone by, and I could notice that Mom was in some dilemma, some pressure. There was definitely something wrong but I couldn't pin down exactly what. I asked her many a time and even insisted and forced her to tell me, but she didn't blurt out a single word. I attempted many a time today in the morning too, but then I had to go to the office. Jay had come to pick me up as usual.

'Hey, gorgeous!' he said, giving me a peck.

'Hey,' I replied in a low and monotonous voice.

'What's wrong, sweetie? Someone's looking very worried and low!' he said, obviously very concerned.

'Nothing much, I just don't know what's wrong with Mom. She looks as if she's in some grave problem from head to toe, but she isn't ready to tell me!' I cried out.

'Ash, just give her some time and some space to contemplate and think over things, and in some time, she herself will tell you when she thinks it is the right time. Just give her some time,' he said very tenderly, trying to soothe me and calm me down.

'Why does she need time, Jay? Why can't she tell me straight away?' I asked irritatingly.

'Well, even I don't have the answer to that, Ash, but I think you should just trust your mom on this and let it be as of now,' he said, sighing.

There was no point in arguing with me, and he knew that, so he pressed me no further.

We went to the office, and the whole damn day, I couldn't concentrate on anything, and all I could think of was what was wrong with Mom. It was the first time she was hiding things from me. At least the first I know. Maybe Jay was right; she'll tell me when she thinks the time is right. There was no point fretting over it now. I was just driving myself crazy, thinking about it again and again.

The office hours got over, and I wanted to go home—to Mom.

'Let's go home, Jay. I need to go home,' I said wearily.

'Aisha, you seem like you are in a clutter. Babe, just give her some time, don't go home and pounce on her!' he said, trying to instil some sense in me.

'But when I go home and see her all worried, I can't resist asking her what has happened!' I said. My head was literally throbbing, and I was at the end of my wits.

'Okay, let's do one thing, don't go home just now. We'll go out somewhere wherein you'll relax and even Auntie will get her space. After I drop you home, I'll talk to her, okay?' he said gently, stroking my hair and patting my back.

I agreed to it, and he took me out for some shopping therapy, and after that, we dined at our favourite Chinese joint, and he came to my place.

'Hi, Mom . . . I am back!' I shouted, opening the door, with Jay following me. But she was nowhere to be seen. Panicking, I frantically started looking everywhere and found her sleeping in her room.

'There she is!' I exclaimed to Jay, heaving a sigh relief.

'Easy, Ash, easy . . .' he said, trying to calm my frenzied nerves.

I went up to Mom and shaking her, I said softly, 'Mom! I and Jay need to talk to you!'

She didn't wake up. I repeated my words thrice and still she didn't come around. I caught her hand, which was now very cold, and it dawned upon me that I was now an orphan.

Mom was no longer in this world; she was dead. Her pulses could not be sensed, and her breathing had stopped.

My mom, the person whom I loved the most in the world, had left me, and now I had no one in this world whom I could call mine. I just stood there silent, frozen, and numbed. Jay supported me and made me sit, and I guess he called his parents as well as the ambulance.

Mom was taken to the hospital, and they declared that she had a severe heart attack around six thirty, which caused her death. Her rituals were finished, and friends from all over poured in. Jay's mom insisted I stay with them at their place, so I was using their guest bedroom.

I just sat in there, never came out. Never felt like coming out. I felt like my whole world had come crashing down. I felt like a rolling stone, without any direction for home, just like a complete unknown who was on her own.

The sweetest part in life is to carry all your memorable memories in life, but the toughest part is staying away from the person who is behind all those memories. In all my memorable memories, my mom was present—those awesome memories with her which will never happen for the second time in my life ever again.

How was I ever gonna live without her? There was no point to my life without her. She was everything to me and meant everything to me. She was my support system, the backbone of my life, and like the body ceases functioning without the spinal cord, my life will too. I can't live without her. There was no way I was gonna live without her. Today I understood that our death is not the greatest loss in life; loss is when life dies inside you while you are alive. My mom was my soul. It was like half of me died when Mom died.

I tried to act normal in front of everyone, but there was always something which reminded me of Mom, and I would start weeping. I couldn't draw a line and move on. There was no way I could do it. Drawing a line after loving someone for twenty-two years is the toughest thing in the world because the weight of the feelings can break that line like a toothpick within no time. I had become vulnerable and weak, just like a helpless victim, sunk deep down into depression, and there was nothing left of me. No trace could be found.

Jay was very concerned, and so were his parents and my other friends. One day his mom came in the room. I looked up but said nothing. She stood there for five long minutes, saying or doing nothing. She suddenly came to me and gave me a tight hug, and I felt as if it was my mom hugging me. I could feel the same warmth, love, and care in Auntie's hug.

'Aisha, darling, please calm down,' she said, consoling and comforting me. Then with a little bit of firmness in her voice, she said, 'Look here, Aisha. Your mom was a strong and independent woman. Don't you think what you are doing is an insult to her and her values in one way?'

'Excuse me? Auntie, I am really sorry, but I didn't get you here,' I said, confused and a bit fed up with people coming in and consoling me.

I hated it because they had no clue of what I was going through! Giving advice is an easy thing after all; following it is the hard part.

'Your mom was one of the strongest women I knew. However and whatever the consequences, she never showed others that she was vulnerable or helpless because she didn't want people to pity her or you. Do you think your condition is gonna please her or honour her values?' she explained as if she was explaining to a whiny and adamant teen.

She made sense. I was behaving in a very childish way. I was running away from my problem, and this was definitely not what my mom taught me. Mom would be absolutely disgusted and embarrassed of my condition if she would have seen me like this. By being depressed and acting like a hapless victim, I was in a way humiliating my mom's principles and her values. That very moment, I decided to behave normal no matter how much pain I will have to take because by behaving like this, I was hurting people close to me as well as my mom and myself, of course.

'Thank you, Auntie. I owe you too much,' I said. The weight of her favour seemed too much on my shoulders now.

'In one second, you termed me as a stranger, didn't you?' she said. Then heaving a sigh, she said, 'Go to office, it will help you divert your attention.' Then she left.

I hadn't quite spent the ideal time with Jay since Mom's death, so I decided to go to him and apologize. He hadn't gone to the office today as he had caught a cold. I went to the kitchen, made some coffee, and went to his room. He was too engrossed in his book to notice I had entered.

'Is it too much to ask for an apology?' I asked, talking in his way.

'Why on earth would you apologize, Ash? For what, may I know?' he asked, keeping the mug aside and pulling me closer to him.

His warmth, the very smell of him, his tenderness while handling me, his love, his lullabies, his smile, his eyes—I had freaking missed every single thing about him.

'For my behaviour, Jay . . . I know I was very unfair towards you. I am so sorry, baby, but I couldn't digest the fact that Mom . . .' I couldn't complete my sentence, my voice started faltering.

'Hey, sweetheart, please settle down. Calm down, Ash!' he said, kissing my hair, and he hugged me.

The hug triggered many feelings, and I started weeping hysterically on his shoulder and started blabbering gibberish, my words incoherent. He carried me to my bedroom, taking my head on his lap, and humming me a lullaby, he put me to sleep.

You do not have to see something to know if it's really there. You just need to believe in it, and I believed that my mom is still alive inside me somehow. It is very hard to stop my heart from loving Mom, as hard as it is to stop the eye from blinking. The more I controlled it, the more it hurt me.

But now I was done with my helplessness. I know it is gonna be very hard, but there's a bright day even after the darkest of dark nights. So no matter how hard it was gonna get, I was gonna stick out my chest, keep my head high, and handle it because that's what Mom would have appreciated.

Chapter 4

It had been months now since Mom's death. Two months to be precise. My life had taken its earlier mundane or exotic (depends upon the individual's choice) routine again. I had learned to create a facade of happiness to hide the sorrow and pain inside me. But there was one person who could definitely see through my facade. It was impossible to deceive him. I was just thinking about Jay when the bell rang.

I had moved back to my place. I opened the door, and there he was standing, looking so good in that crisp white shirt and light-blue denims—the light colours adding more quality to his fairness and features and those impeccable grey eyes looking as deep as ever. Even though I was in so much pain, I was affected by him so much. Ah! Wonders of love . . .

'Hey, love . . .' he said, holding my hand and coming inside. 'You remember about the party tonight, right?'

In the evening, there was a party to celebrate the success of Yash's second book. Yash is Jay's elder brother, who is, I guess, two years older than us. He was never interested in the family business but was a very creative person and always wanted to become an author.

'Yeah, I do remember,' I said, smiling and kissing him. Kissing him makes me feel dizzy. I go in a fantasy world, and it is really difficult to come back.

He started chuckling, seeing my expressions. Then with a stupid childish grin, he asked, 'My love, I have brought you a dress, will you wear it tonight?'

For that smile, I'll do anything. Wearing a dress is a very small thing to do. Without even opening the dress, I said, 'Aye aye, Captain!' and gave him a huge grin.

Time passed in talks, romance, and as usual, he brought a smile on my face. I don't know how he manages to do so, but every time we meet, he manages to make me smile from the bottom of my heart. Usually with others I just fake a smile, and he could always see through that fake me, but when with him, I smile wholeheartedly. Without humour, life is boring. Without love, life is hopeless. And without Jay, my life is impossible.

At around five, I opened the gift-wrapped box which contained the dress I was gonna wear tonight at the party. It was a very pretty dress, and it looked very expensive. I told him not to spend so recklessly on me, but he never seemed to listen. I abhorred the fact he spent so much on me, but then money is next to nothing when it comes to the Singhania family.

Sighing, I took out the metallic grey one-piece. It was so beautiful; more than beautiful, it was mesmerizing—a dress which was designed to grab eyeballs and was meant to grab the spotlight. Ah! God only knows what goes on in that guy's head.

I put on the dress and matched it with metallic grey-and-black heels, dark-grey shimmery studs, metallic grey necklace, and a black watch. I made up my hair by tying them up in a way very similar to the French roll. I was ready, and the next minute, I could hear his car rolling inside my gate and that familiar honk of his car.

He hadn't come to pick me up. He had sent his driver.

'Where is Jay, Uncle?' I asked him.

'Jay sir busy, so I come,' he said and started driving.

I reached by 6.30 p.m., and Yash was the one who greeted me.

'Good evening, Aisha,' he said.

Jay and Yash were very close to each other. They were brothers-cum-best friends. They shared everything with each other and were always updated about each other's life no matter what they were doing or where they were.

'Good evening. Congratulations for your book,' I said, appreciating his efforts.

'Ah! Thank you so much,' he said, smiling. Then with a serious expression on his face, he asked, 'You are serious about him, aren't you?'

'I am very much serious about your brother, Yash, as serious as he is about me,' I said, trying to make him believe me. I have no idea as to why he asked me that question out of the blue. Frankly, the question offended me.

'Don't mind me asking you that. It's just that he was hurt beyond limits on many occasions due to you. I am not saying that it was your fault or something. I know you never knew about his feelings. I just wanted to confirm. Pardon me if you were even the slightest bit hurt,' he said, and with each word, I realized the intensity of their relationship.

'I never knew about his feelings, Yash. I was cruel to even myself. I loved him since I was sixteen, but like, he never had it in him to tell me, neither did I,' I said, trying not to lose my composure. Oh God! Why in the heck am I so emotional?

'Sixteen? Aisha Mukherjee, you loved me since you were sixteen, and you never told me this!' exclaimed Jay, his tone shocked.

'Where did you come from?' I asked a bit taken aback due to the sudden and unannounced entry of the guy I love.

'That really doesn't matter! You loved me since you were sixteen? What does that mean?' he asked. His eyes were very eager and hungry to know the answer, and he seemed annoyed yet pleased with the information.

'I will, er, leave the two of you alone,' Yash said and left, giving the two of us some privacy.

'Answer me before I go mad, Ash!' he said, his expressions showing he had no more patience.

Taking a deep breath, I said, 'Yes, I loved you since I was sixteen. I realized this on my birthday, during our 10th grade exams.'

Taking my face in his hands, he said very gently, 'Why did you never tell me then, and what about the guy whom you dated in Paris—Chris?'

'I never told you because you never seemed interested in me, and you always flirted with every pretty gal, and as far as dating Chris was concerned, I dated him only to get over you and also because he had the same features as you had,' I said, a bit embarrassed, but it was getting difficult to breathe.

'Oh Lord God! I was gonna ask you out when you had returned to India for the two-month vacation, but then I heard about Chris, and I thought you really loved him, so

I never uttered a word, and then to distract myself and also to get over you, I dated Shanaya!' he said, and then shaking his head in a negative manner, he continued, 'What fools we are, Ash!'

Laughing over our stupidity, sighing over the misunderstandings, and thinking of what could have been, we went inside the club 'cause Yash was about to deliver his address. His address was fantastic, which was obvious given the fact that he is a splendid writer.

'My brother here, Jay, wishes to surprise everyone here now except for, obviously, me,' he said, winking mischievously with an ecstatic gleam in his eyes, and he had a very notorious grin on his face.

I wondered what it could be. Jay never told me anything. Maybe it wasn't related to me or wasn't that important. Anyways, he left my hand and went on the stage.

Taking the mike from Yash's hand, he said, 'Today I am here to do something, say something special to someone special!'

Everyone started cheering, and I went red. I mean, at least I thought it was gonna be for me. Oops, or it can even be for Yash, but then Yash already knew, right? Ugh! Why do I think so much?

'Aisha, could you please come up?' he asked, his voice ringing all over the club, giving me a shrill.

I blushed, a deep-red one at that, when all eyes turned to me as I went up the stage. Now I understood the mystery behind the eye-grabbing dress. But the motive was yet not found.

I went up on the stage and grabbing a box out of his back pocket, he went down on one knee and said, 'Aisha

Mukherjee, will you marry me?' He opened the box and pulled out a ring, waiting for my answer.

I was in a state of amusement and bewilderment—shocked and silent. Even now, I was so surprised that my mind was in one world and my heart in some other. Love is life, and as they say, if you miss out on love, then you miss out on life, and my answer was very obvious to the people who knew us, and for those who didn't, my expressions were more than enough to show my innermost feelings.

'I love you, a lot . . . and my answer is so obviously yes! It will be an honour, Jay!' I said, tears flowing out of my eyes, tears of happiness. I swear to God this was the best day of my existence.

I still couldn't believe I was Jay Singhania's fiancée. Dreams do come true. A confession is all it takes, and then you get a new birth. You start a new life, and here the very same thing was happening. I was grabbing, or, for want of a better word, hugging the extra lifeline I was getting. It was really a dream come true. My dream had got its wings. I was soon gonna become Mrs Jay Singhania. I still remember the scrawling behind my notebooks, 'Aisha Singhania' written all over the back page, and I loved the ring of Aisha Singhania. I loved it, totally did.

Love is the great miraculous cure. It works like miracles in our lives. This made me forget all the problems, all the sorrows, and all the pains in my life. Jay always strikes at the right time. He knows exactly when I need him the most. Jay has put up with my worst behaviour and has been exceptionally affectionate even when I have been extremely irritable. He never ceased to believe in me even when I had stopped believing in myself. He has accepted me with all my faults like the earth withholds all its beings, and he has always loved me just the way I am.

I believed in Jay and his love for me from the bottom of my heart. Every part of my body knows and always knew the audacity of his love and what limits it could cross for me. My soul knew the intensity of his love for me and how deep it could go, and my heart knew the magnitude of his love and how much more it could expand and still can.

Nothing feels better than when you love someone with your whole heart and soul and they love you back even more. There was celebration all around and love was in the air. Parties were thrown, functions were conducted, and I couldn't wait any more to announce it to the whole world that I was gonna marry Jay.

Jay never demanded much and never complained and never expected much, never! He loved me without expectations, and I loved him without limitations, and when I first met Jay, I never ever in my wildest dreams dreamed that he would mean the world for me one day.

Life is all about finding magic in unexpected and non-clichéd places and things and falling in love with unexpected people at unexpected times. I never expected to fall in love with Jay, and falling for him during our tenth grade exams was hilariously stupid and unexpected!

The Singhania family was a renowned one in the city and a respected and admired one at that. Jay's parents were very happy with the recent happenings and were more than glad to accept me as their daughter-in-law. According to them, I was already like their daughter to them, and these words meant the world to me. I mean, I had feared his parents' reaction to this somehow. You never know what can happen when it comes to the psyche of Indian parents on their offspring's wedding!

The wedding had been announced, and the invitations had been sent to all. The preparations were in full swing, and with the passing of every day, my dream of becoming Mrs Jay Singhania was coming closer! Jay had taken me out on a date that night, and there were around four more weeks to go for the wedding. We were sitting in a five-star hotel.

'You are looking breathtakingly and heartbreakingly beautiful today!' he exclaimed, smiling, his smile making me blush.

'So every day I look just ordinary, eh?' I asked, trying to pull his leg.

But then he suddenly got serious, and with intense seriousness and maturity in his voice, he said, 'You're no ordinary mortal in my life. You are immortal for me. No one can replace you, my angel. No one can! My life without you was like a sky without the twinkling, brilliance and bright light of the stars and when you entered, everything was illuminated—my life was—and everything shone out, and there was lustre and radiance everywhere!'

Those words meant so much to me. We all need a little help sometimes. We need someone to help us hear the musical language in the world, someone to make us realize our worth, someone to make us feel prized, someone to cherish us, someone to help us through the darkness which the light can't invade, and someone to remind us that it always won't be this way and that things will change. That someone is out there right in front of me. That someone in my life is Jay.

It was just fourteen days to go for the wedding, and that day we were in the office. I had gone to meet the German clients and was back by about two. I entered Jay's cabin, and I could smell rats. Something was wrong, very wrong.

'Jay? What's wrong? Tell me!' I asked, very frightened. I had never seen Jay like this, so serious as if there was something major which had gone wrong!

'Do you remember Ashwin?' he asked very calmly.

'He is the same guy who was working with you on the new model in New York, which was your brainchild right?' I replied back, being very precise.

'Yes,' he replied as if he was depleted of all the energy in his body.

'Okay, so what about him, Jay? Will you please tell me what has happened for God's sake?' I replied, irritated now.

'He did land fraud and took away as good as forty crore from our account, and now he is missing,' he said, trying to be as calm as possible, but his tone was a total giveaway!

Now I could understand what was going through his mind! Forty crore gone with a wedding—our wedding—in a week! Damn it!

'So now with our wedding in fourteen days, are we gonna face police and investigations and stuff?' I asked, still concerned only about the wedding.

'Aisha. I need to tell you something,' he said. Now his voice was as grave as ever, and I could sense he was in immense pain.

'What is it? Something more in that Ashwin matter?' I asked.

'It was my project, and I chose Ashwin, and hence I need to go to New York and sort things out. We need to cancel the wedding, Ash!' he said, and he couldn't look into my eyes while he said that.

The last sentence brought my whole world crashing down. I couldn't speak, wasn't able to say anything.

'So you don't wanna marry me?' I asked, my nose red due to crying and my eyes swollen a bit.

'When did I say I don't wanna marry you, baby! All I am saying is, let's just postpone the wedding! That's it!' he said, annoyed.

'That's it? Jay Singhania, do you realize there are only two freaking weeks left for the wedding? All the invitations have been sent, all the arrangements have been done!' I shrieked, tears streaming down my cheeks.

'I have no other option, Aisha! I love you, and I have been waiting for eons to marry you. It's not like I am not hurt!' he said, his voice cracking and breaking.

'I knew you never wanted to marry me! You're a Casanova after all! All these are just reasons!' I said, banging my fist on the table.

'Ash, take it easy, please. I am not saying I am cancelling the wedding. All I am saying is that let's just postpone it,' he replied, not really in his senses, his eyes almost red, and he seemed vulnerable.

'Why can't you finish off with the wedding and then go to New York?' I asked, trying to catch him in his words and trying to develop a solution.

'Are you out of your senses, Aisha? Every day the money is going, and I need to get to the sight, look into the matter, stop the losses, find the guy, and get the money back!' he said, visualizing the uphill task.

'Why don't you just say you don't wanna marry me and stop lying?' I said sarcastically, and going out, I banged the door on his face.

I took my things and went home straight, not wanting to make a scene in the office. I didn't wanna meet anyone because I felt humiliated and insulted that Jay was cancelling the wedding, especially after the whole world knowing we were gonna get married. I cried myself to sleep as I was feeling dizzy.

I woke up at around six in the evening, and I found Jay sitting on the corner of my bed, watching me. I didn't say a word, not wanting to argue with him, and got out of the bed.

'C'mon, Ash, now this is childishness! You have to understand me. The situation demands this. I wanna get married to you as much as you want to, in fact more than you want to! So stop all this please!' he said, and he had annoyance written all over his face.

'If you get so irritated by me, why marry me? Just do whatever the hell you want. I am no one to stop you,' I said, my words as cold as ice.

'Enough of all this please! You are acting as if I am not gonna marry you or something!' he said, and he was clearly pissed and was barely able to keep his anger in control.

'Are you? I am no longer sure of that answer now, Sir Jay,' I said, referring to him as my boss in the office and no more my boyfriend or even my friend.

'I am leaving for New York tomorrow evening, baby doll . . .' he said, coming closer to me and holding my hand.

'Go, Jay. Please leave before I do something to you. You and I, we end here, Jay Singhania! Get lost!' I bellowed, shivering due to anger and crying on the verge of fainting.

He left my house and me alone in a state of complete blankness and sorrow. I was heart-broken, completely heart-broken. Nothing seemed right! Everything was going wrong. My life which was perfect some hours ago had turned into a living nightmare. Reality, as we interpret in a biased way, is a greater illusion than the dream world, and somehow these words made complete sense to me.

We can give without loving, but we cannot love without giving, and I had given each and every part of my heart, soul, and brain to that guy who cancelled the wedding for a business problem! Is that my value in his life? My entire freaking world revolves around him! He's the centre of my universe, and my life without him would be like the solar system without the sun—unimaginable and impossible! I just broke up with my own sun. How was I ever gonna manage without him? How will I live without him? And even if I do survive, will that life be worth living?

A week had passed since this whole drama took place. Before leaving, Jay had come home again to persuade me, but I refused to even meet him. I didn't even wish to see his face no matter how breathtakingly beautiful it may be! Tejaswini, Karishma, Nehal, and Pranita had tried reasoning me out of my decision, but their tactics and arguments were up to no avail.

Tejaswini had come over that day. She was worried sick about me. Caressing my hair, she said, 'What is the point of torturing yourself as well as him, darling?'

'I am not torturing myself, and he is the one who called off the wedding, not me!' I said, pain reflecting in every word of mine.

'See, Aisha, you as well as I know you love him like anything, and you know he loves you with the same intensity and affection, if not more. It is a huge thing, sweetie, the New York blow! It was mandatory for him to go, and if he had any other option, he would have never called off the wedding, and you know that very well!' she said, still hoping I would back off on that harsh decision of mine.

'I don't wanna talk about all this shit now, and I back my decision wholeheartedly,' I said, pretending not to care about all the mess.

'Decisions made in haste and when you are in a state of anger and pain, they never give good results, Aisha, that's all I wanna say. Whatever decision you take, I am with you in it, babe. You jump, I jump, remember?' she said, hugging me tight.

'I love you, and that surely means a lot,' I said.

'I love you too, Aisha, no matter how stupid your decision may be! Now let's just sleep, can we? I am darn sleepy!' she said, giving a big yawn.

We both started laughing, and she went to sleep while I couldn't because of all those thoughts going over and over in my head, driving me insane!

I loved Jay even now, more than anything, but I couldn't digest the fact that he called off our wedding. I mean, couldn't he just finish off with that and then go? But I guess I am not that important to him any more. My heart was ready to forgive him even now, but it was my brain that was angry, and it was the ruling party.

The next day, I was discussing a project with Ileana when Jay's dad entered my cabin. He gestured her to leave us alone.

After she closed the door, he let out a sigh and then said, 'It was very important and necessary and urgent for him to go there as soon as possible. It was not his fault all this happened, Aisha! He was more excited and intent on marrying you than you were. I am not here to force you to change your decision or something like that. Just here for us to get the facts straight and also because it concerns the happiness of my son and my daughter as well.'

'Uncle, you have to understand my position as well. Try fitting into my boots, and you'll understand the amount of pain and humiliation I am facing now!' I said, trying to control my tears.

'Aisha, hard times come in every relationship, and every couple has to cross some obstacles. Life is not a bed of roses after all! You need to fight these obstacles together! Both of you have to!' he said, and he seemed drained out and dull.

'But there are some things that have to be given top priority, and if someone goofs up over there, making the other one fall down on her face, problems are bound to be created!' I argued back, trying to keep my manners intact and not raising my voice.

'I tried explaining to both of you. Now what you both do is upon you two, best of luck,' he said and left my cabin.

I was annoyed and frustrated and fired up! Uncle thought I was the one at fault! Why couldn't somebody just see through my point of view? I had no one in this world to call mine, and this wedding was called off by the Singhanias, and that too only two weeks prior to the wedding. Wasn't it very obvious that people would think that there is some fault in me? That there is something wrong with me? I am not properly suited for one of the heir's of the Singhania property, and hence, the wedding had been called off! I was the one being portrayed as the bad person in the minds of people, and I can't take that, especially knowing that I have no family as such of mine! It makes me more and more insecure and even vulnerable for that matter.

Before leaving for home, I went to Uncle's cabin and said, 'I really appreciate your efforts, Uncle, and I am really sorry if any of my words or actions have hurt you. Believe me, they weren't intentional.'

'I understand, Aisha, and take care of yourself. You seem weak,' he said, shaking his head.

'I will. Thanks,' I said, managing to give him a meek smile, and hopped out of his cabin.

I went home and, not caring to have dinner, went to my room and jumped on my bed inside my blanket. I felt so insecure. The world outside was so dark and bad. I wanted him by my side; I needed him by my side. I wish Jay could be here.

I wonder what is going on over there. Would he be missing me? I wonder what he must be doing there right now, and I still ponder over whether he actually is depressed that he had to call off the wedding. Does he think about me there, or with the cold weather, even his heart has been roofed up by ice? Does he still love me, or now he just doesn't give a damn?

Even after all this, I still love him and care for him as much as I did before. Maybe even more, but definitely not less because once you care for a person, you will always do the same. What's in your mind may change, but what's in your heart will remain forever, always and forever . . .

Jay had come back to India for two days due to some file and signature confusion. I had no clue that he was in India until he popped up at my place.

I had taken a shower, and my hair was still pretty wet. I was exhausted after the day's work and was having orange juice when he entered.

'Aish, how are you?' he asked wearily, and it seemed pretty apparent that he hadn't slept properly for days altogether.

'Why do you ask?' I asked, still wondering and even worrying about the reason behind the dark circles below his eyes.

'Damn it, Aisha. Because I bloody care for you and I love you, and get that straight in your head!' he said, clearly annoyed beyond limits, but his tone was weary, and it looked like he had no energy in him to do anything.

'If you need to be reminded, then I better remind you that we are no longer together and the—' I was continuing when he came up to me and started kissing me, his kiss getting hungrier every minute.

I tried pushing him off, but my physical strength was nowhere in comparison with him, and all my will of pushing him off was curbed down when the kiss grew passionate. Ah! I love him so much. All the pain, anger, and frustration of all these days we spent apart could be sensed in the kiss, and we couldn't end it in a kiss, and that night I lost one thing which mattered more than anything to me and which was intact for years and years altogether—my virginity.

He was still sleeping when I got up. What happened last night wasn't right. I hooked up with the guy who cancelled our wedding; he is the same guy who is behind the excruciating pain I am suffering right now! Last night I committed the biggest mistake of my life. I was frustrated and angry, but I couldn't blame him for anything. Whatever happened happened with my consent, and with the flow we were in, it would be a crime to break it. It all seemed so perfect and so nice until today.

'Do you still need any proof for our love?' he asked me. He was up when I was deeply engrossed in my own thoughts.

'What happened yesterday was a mistake. It was not love, Jay, it was lust, and there's a huge difference between the two,' I said, trying to somehow control myself and seem firm in front of him because if he saw any loopholes, he will know exactly how to use them to convince me.

'Fine then, Aisha Mukherjee, I rest my case here now! I am tired of explaining my side to you now. One of the basic things in a relationship is understanding, which we don't seem to have. You think I am a mistake then, so be it, Aisha!' he said, his tone was coated up with sarcasm and his words lethal—lethal 'cause they killed me the instant they came out of his mouth.

Those words pierced my heart like a thousand needles had been inserted into that sweet little red-shaped thing which beats only for one guy, but the same guy just mauled up the same heart wherein he resided with ferocity and cruelty. It was a big blow to our relationship—a final blow to Jay &Aisha.

It had been two weeks since then, and I had tried behaving normal, but it wasn't possible for me. That day I had lost two of the most important things in my life—my virginity and Jay—and I wasn't getting either back. Mom, Dad, and Jay were the most important people in my life, and I had lost all three in succession.

If there's one thing that I've learned, then that is if you love until it hurts, there can be no more hurt, only more love. And I loved Jay with all my mind, heart, body, and soul, and I was happy just loving him. I realized his value in my life after I lost him. Like they say, the value of something is seldom known until it is lost.

I had been ill for some days now, and hence, I decided to visit the doctor that day. I had my appointment at five thirty, and I was waiting in her cabin when Dr Sharma arrived.

'Hey there, Aisha, seen you after years!' she said. She was our family doctor for years now, and she knew me since I was a kid.

'Yeah, I was studying in France,' I said, giving her a timid smile.

'So I heard,' she said, and then getting straight to the point, she asked, 'So what's wrong with you?'

'I don't know. I have been vomiting, sleeping too much, getting tired easily, etc.,' I answered.

She checked my pulse rate and stuff, and then she looked at me, her face solemn and grave. Her look kinda disturbed me.

'What's wrong?' I asked, a bit scared and wishing Jay could be here.

'Aisha . . . You are, er . . .' she said, not really able to complete it. But then taking a deep breath, she said, 'You are pregnant, Aisha.'

I just sat there, unmoving and silent. Not really thinking and not really in my senses, I murmured a thank you and left.

Holy crap! I was pregnant! I was carrying Jay's child—Jay and my child. I still hadn't come to terms with the fact that I was single and, on the top of it, pregnant! It is a taboo in the Indian society, and for the first time in my entire life, I was this frightened and scared. I had no one in this entire world that I could call family. I couldn't possibly tell this to anyone—anyone but Jay. But there was no way I was telling him about this! I don't want him on these terms; I don't want him to marry me because he doesn't have any other option. No, there was no way I was gonna tell him this. I don't want his sympathy and certainly not his pity.

The very next day, I gave my resignation letter and vacated my post. I had no idea what to do about the baby or whom to tell! I was thinking about it when the doorbell rang. I opened the door to a person whom I would never in my most insane dreams imagine to be standing on my front door.

'What on heaven's sake are you doing here, Yash?' I asked, stupefied and stunned.

'Er, can I come in first?' he asked, a bit embarrassed and uncomfortable.

'Oh, pardon me, I am very sorry. Please come in,' I said, biting my tongue.

'Thanks,' he said, a bit curt, and that offended me in a way, but then I chose to ignore it.

'Yash, if you have come to talk about the wedding, then please let it be. It's of no use,' I said, being frank.

'Can't I just come here as a friend?' he asked.

'Yeah of course you can drop in any time,' I said, trying to fake a smile. *Yeah as if!* I thought ironically.

'I heard you left the job . . .' his voice trailed in my living room. I had no clue as to why and what Yash was doing here. Maybe Jay had sent him to clear things.

'Oh yeah, that is because I need some time off,' I said my answers to the point.

The talks went on, and as time passed, both of us grew quite comfortable of each other's company. It was 9 p.m. when he left. I had a good time with him. He helped me divert my attention, but I still hadn't found any solution to that sword hanging on my head. If only Jay had never cancelled the wedding, all these problems wouldn't have been there.

I was missing him so much, and all those memories of us were coming back and haunting me. Those long talks about everything and anything, having fun and frolic yet having discussions of sensibility and career, those memories wherein we stood by each other no matter what, the moments wherein I cried, he consoled, we cared—those memories are treasured deeply in the heart of my soul.

Sometimes it's not only the horrible or the bad memories that make you sad but also the best ones—the most memorable and remarkable memories which you know will never happen for the second time in your life because the person who was behind those memories and responsible for the memories left that responsibility as well as you alone forever and ever.

Chapter 5

Yash dropped by the next day as well and the day after as well. Days turned into weeks, and Yash without fail turned up on my doorstep every day. We started getting closer with each passing day, and it had become a part of my routine to meet him now. The real problem was yet not solved, and the slight bump on my stomach was now slightly noticeable. It had been four weeks since I had come to know about my pregnancy.

My mood swings were creepy, and I was very scared. I was crying uncontrollably that day when Yash entered.

'Hey, babe, what's wrong?' he asked patting my shoulder and trying to shush me.

'I am pregnant, Yash!' I said, finally letting it out to someone.

'Is Jay the father?' he asked, and he himself was astounded by the news.

'Is that even a question to ask?' I exclaimed exasperatingly.

'Sorry, sorry, sorry!' he chanted. 'Does he even know about all this? I don't think he does, does he?'

'No, he doesn't,' I said, choking on my own words.

'Call him this instant and tell him everything! He deserves to know!' Yash said in a very governing tone.

'I won't tell him that I am pregnant. I'll tell him I wanna meet him and talk about something. I don't want him to marry me out of guilt or sympathy!' I replied, sounding very firm and obdurate.

'Okay, fine, but please call this minute,' he begged, and it looked as if the news had hit him bad because his expressions puzzled me. I couldn't make head or tail out of them.

That very instant, I called Jay and said, 'I need to talk to you.'

He replied in a very curt and rude manner, and his reply consisted of just one sentence, 'No, can't, busy,' and he hung up on me. This reply confirmed my fear that I was just a toy for the playboy.

Yash heard our conversation and saw how deep down I was into trouble.

'What are you gonna do about the baby, Aisha?' he asked, very concerned.

'I have no idea,' I said and started weeping hysterically.

He took me into his arms and tried consoling me.

He held my chin and made me look up, and in very gentle words, he asked, 'Will you marry me, Aisha?'

I couldn't believe my ears! I respected this guy from the core of my heart because of his goodness, and this is what he does—ask his brother's ex-girlfriend or, better word, ex-fiancée to marry him? This was absolutely disgustingly and humorously ridiculous!

'How dare you, Yash? How could you even think that way? I love Jay from the bottom of my heart, and the sooner you get it the better!' I shrieked in disbelief.

'Aisha Mukherjee, will you please give me one chance to explain?' he implored.

'This better be good, Yash!' I said and gave him a bad, hard stare.

'I, as it is, don't stay here and am usually in Bangalore. You marry me, your child will get a name, and you'll be safe and won't be a target for the gossipmongers. I won't deny the fact that I love you, but I won't even touch you without your consent,' he said softly, stroking my hair.

I felt like I was standing in some typical Bollywood masala film with a love triangle between the hero, heroine, and the villain, but I was just not sure who the villain was in here.

Jay was the guy I loved who left me, and Yash was a guy whom I respected and admired and he was the one who was standing by me in my testing and intricate times. But the fact that I was hurting both these darlings of mine, in a way, literally killed me from the inside, and I felt sick and disgusting!

'Yash, why are you ruining your life for me? I can't let you do this. I am sorry. You are a darling, but I can't be that selfish! I mean, c'mon, you will get any girl you want, gals better than me!' I said, my head throbbing badly, and I was on the verge of fainting.

'But what if the gal I want is you? Aisha, why do you think after Shwetha I had no girlfriend? Because I fell in love with you. I am either gonna marry you or no one, and I would be honoured to father your and Jay's child, and c'mon, it's my duty to keep you safe!' he said, leaving no stone unturned in convincing me.

'What the hell? Shwetha was your ex! Why didn't she ever tell me about it?' I asked, but then realized that there was a more important topic on hold. 'What about Jay, and then what about your parents?' I asked, trying to put down my point properly.

'You don't have to worry about any of it. I'll juggle all of it,' he said and then hugged me.

The next few hours, he kept stressing on the advantages of our wedding, telling me how much both of us would benefit from it—especially me—and how everything would be in accordance to my wishes. He was not giving me time to contemplate over things. He wanted quick answers and he was pressuring me for them and I was confused, very confused with no family of my own. I could no longer take anything and finally succumbed to his proposal.

'Aisha, trust me, you have no idea how exulted I am today, my ecstasy has crossed its limits and is over the sky now. I love you so much, I can't tell you how much. No words can justify my love and the intensity of my love for you. I love you with a love that is more than love, and if there's one thing I can assure you, then that is, not one drop of water will come out of these beautiful brown eyes of yours!' he said, looking intensely in my eyes, and his words and the look in his eyes somehow convinced me that this guy truly loves me from the bottom of his heart.

But I had to keep the mirror in front of him, and hence I replied, 'But I love Jay, and no matter what, I will continue to love Jay, and it won't be fair to you, Yash, that I marry you when I love your brother.'

'Love is not always about possession, Aisha,' he replied. 'For me, love is about appreciation.'

I was silent after that reply. I didn't know whether to consider myself fortunate or unfortunate. One brother desolated me and left me and my life hanging on a thread while the other brother is handling the thread and is giving the thread the strength to multiply and form strings to save itself at the cost of his happiness and life. Amazing! How complicated can someone's life be? I was a living example to the answer of this question.

'Jay?' I choked. I had no clue how Jay was gonna react if he came to know this.

'Don't worry, Ash. We won't have a grand celebration. No one has to know except for my parents. It will be a simple court marriage. Is that fine by you?' he asked. He had very meticulously planned everything, taking care of every detail.

'Hmm,' I said as that was all I could say after all this.

I was still in shock, and I was scared as hell just imagining what Jay's reaction is gonna be after he comes to know all this. I won't be able to handle if he starts hating me or something like that. It was very obvious that this news is at least gonna give him currents, if not pain. I felt very sick and disgusting when I deeply started contemplating the outcomes of this wedding. I was ruining Yash's life by marrying him, and I knew it to the very core that I was aware of it, but then I had no other option.

'Worrying about Jay, eh?' he asked me, and I could see that the fact that I loved Jay pricked him even though he never mentioned it.

'Thank you, Yash, thank you so much. I don't know what I would have done without you. I can't thank you enough . . .' I said, expressing every ounce of gratitude I had towards him.

'Don't thank me, Ash. There should not be awe and gratitude in love,' he said, giving me a peck on my cheek.

Ash . . . Only Jay used to call me Ash, and only he had the right to call me that. I quite didn't like the fact that Yash was calling me that, but then I already owe the guy a lot. He has sacrificed almost everything for me, so I let it be.

He lived in hope; hope that one fine day he'll replace Jay in my life, which was impossible no matter what happened. Tomorrow even if Jay hates me, I would still love that guy, love him like no one can ever love him or has ever loved him. No one can love him like I do. I never felt this defenceless as I feel just now without Jay. We are never that defenceless against sufferings as we are when we love.

'Are you okay with the date, sweetie?' he asked me between some calls.

I and Yash were gonna get married this very Sunday, and his parents were informed about the marriage, and very obviously, they were fantastically and vastly against it.

'I don't have any problem with anything, Yash,' I said, and the thought that I was gonna get married to Yash was still not penetrating.

'So long, so good,' he said, smiling and going back to his calls, dreaming of a different world and that sentence so reminded me of the guy who owns my heart, my soul, and my brain—Jay.

My heart was not ready to move on; my heart was not ready to marry Yash. It was Jay; it always was Jay whom I dreamed in that frame of my wedding picture. It was one idea which was inescapable. He is everything I want, everything I desire, and everything I dream of. He is not only my star; he is my entire freaking sky with the stars.

'What are you thinking of?' Yash asked. 'By the way, you remember about the appointment with the court person to decide the time and all, right?'

'Yeah, yeah, I do remember. Don't worry,' I said, trying to keep Jay and his thoughts at bay.

Yash came forward and held my hand. He pulled me close. I was getting uncomfortable. No one in the world except for Jay can do that. He sensed my frustration and discomfort and let go of me.

'Yash, are you sure about what we are doing?' I asked, not quite able to meet his gaze, which was full of adoration.

'I had to try, at least once, but I must say he has got his claws deep down into you,' he said, banging the door and upsetting the frames hung besides the door.

This was expected from Yash. I mean, c'mon, he is human after all. He has feelings, desires, and needs which have to be fulfilled, and I was neither in the condition nor the state to fulfil either of them, and nor was I capable of devoting myself to him. How much more could he possibly sacrifice for me?

Every person has both good and bad in him. No matter how good a man seems, he has some evil. And no matter how bad a man seems, there's something good about him.

'I am, er, sorry about what happened in the afternoon. I really am, and believe me, it won't happen again,' Yash said, embarrassed, while I was leaving for home.

'I am not angry, Yash. It's totally all right, and *you* are doing me a favour by marrying me, not vice versa, so take it easy. I need to get home. Take care of yourself, and lemme know what happens at the court,' I said. Not really wanting to give him wrong signals, I left for home.

After reaching home, I had this enormous urge of talking to Jay and telling him about the excruciating pain I was going through—to tell him how much it hurt me to stay apart from him and to tell him that it literally kills me that we, I and he, don't talk any more, but then I think, if my love wasn't enough, will my words even matter? Thinking so, I tried diverting my attention back to making coffee.

'You look so cute when you are deep into your thoughts, I love observing you when you think,' he said, looking merry with an enthusiastic gleam in his eyes.

'What's the matter with you? What's the reason behind the exuberant smile, huh?' I asked, giving him a cup of coffee.

'There are three reasons,' he said, still smiling broadly. 'You, our marriage, and you again. All three reasons have "Aisha" written over them.'

I had no clue how to react. I was at a loss of words. I mean, I am going to marry Yash, but I was used to hearing such love-filled sentences only from Jay, his brother. Fabulous, isn't it?

Sensing I had nothing to retort back, he said, 'One day, Aisha Mukherjee, you will love me, and that's a promise I make to you, and I swear by it.'

'Yash, no . . .' I was about to reply, but he was out of the door by then.

We are gonna get married in three days, and I still wasn't sure whether what I was doing was right or wrong. I was in two minds. One mind wanted to tell Jay that I loved him even now and that I was pregnant, and the other mind was in accordance to what Yash had said and promised.

I was going through the worst phase of my life, and there was this question which haunted me like anything: 'Does Jay love me even now?' But I had this huge ego, which wouldn't let me ask him that. There's this bug that comes out of nowhere and everywhere and starts eating my head with the same question which neither I nor my heart has any answers to.

It was the day of my wedding, and Jay's mom had dressed me up. She looked exhausted and pale and dull. She wasn't really happy with the fact that I was messing up the lives of both her sons.

I had no clue to what I was doing; I had lost touch with what was going on in my life. Frankly putting it, I was just lost, and I was using Yash as a light to guide me through the darkness or maybe the light to my new future.

'We just have to sign here, and then it's all done. We will be officially announced married,' Yash said, handing me the paper.

Taking the paper from his hand, I said, 'Okay, that is it then . . .'

He took the papers; the person who had the legal rights to announce us as a couple did so. Something was stamped on a paper, and we were declared married. That one piece of paper ended everything between me and my love; it ended everything between me and Jay.

We went home, and our bags were already packed. We had our flight to Bangalore in two hours. Auntie was like my second mom, and I couldn't bear that look on her face.

While leaving, I held her hand and said, 'I don't know whether what I am doing is morally correct or not, but I'll promise you one thing, I will do my best to keep Yash happy.

I'll try my level best, and I promise you, I'll take good care of him. You can trust me.'

'It's not about trusting you, sweetheart. You love Jay, and everyone knows that. How will you be able to keep Yash happy and stay married to him when your heart lies with his younger brother? And do you think after knowing this entire thing, Jay won't be infuriated? You know him pretty well, Aisha . . . I'll leave the rest up to you,' she said, her eyes moist and her tone filled with concern over her two sons who had fallen for the same gal.

I went to the airport with a heavy heart and a confused mind. I decided that very moment I would fulfil my promise; I will try my best to keep Yash and my child happy. Now they are my new world; now they are my new life. It was a new beginning, and I was gonna start it anew. I owed that to Yash.

'Our flight is on schedule. We have to go through the customs. Let's move then?' Yash said, checking if we had our tickets and the other necessary documents.

'Yash, I don't know how much I owe you and the only terms in which I can ever give you back are love, affection, and understanding. I'll never be able to love you like I love Jay, but I love you for the guy you are, and I respect you for the humanity inside you. I'll do whatever it takes to make you happy,' I said, giving him a tight hug.

'I love you, Aish, more than anything in the world and more than anyone else in the world, and I am more than happy to marry you and give my name to your and Jay's child. No one in the world has to know it is Jay's child because I'll love that child like my own,' he said lovingly.

The darkest night is often the bridge to the brightest tomorrow. This was the night of my ending, and tomorrow I would precede my new beginning—my new beginning in Bangalore, my new beginning with my husband and soon-to-be-coming child. I had to delete Jay for that, delete every trace and evidence of his existence in my life because I had promised to devote myself totally to Yash and my child, my sweet yet-to-be-born child.

It was the start of a new chapter in my life. The most beautiful part of this chapter is letting go of the past, letting go of those mistakes I made, and letting go of those memories which still haunt me, letting go of all the things I did, received, went through and made others go through in their life.

I promised not to repeat those mistakes committed and confidently enter this new chapter with a mixture of experience and anticipation. Anticipating that I will make this chapter preponderant than the earlier one and maybe one of the most ideal and memorable chapter in the book of my life.

Chapter 6

'I am leaving for my seminar. I'll come home late in the evening, maybe by seven. I'll drop Ayaan to school on the way. Bye, darling, take care. I love you more than I love myself,' he said, winking at me.

'Bye. You too take care,' I told him and gave him a hug, and turning to Ayaan, I said, 'Behave yourself, li'l boy. Remember, Momma loves you more than anyone else. Take care of yourself, baby, I'll come and pick you up after school ends, okay?'

'Okay, Mom. I love you too,' he said, and giving me a peck on my cheek, he left with Yash.

It had been seven years since my and Yash's marriage, and I had given birth to the most charming and handsome boy. We had named him Ayaan, which means the gift of God, and true to his name, he was a gift of God for me and Yash, a blessing in our lives.

Ayaan was so mesmerizing that you couldn't get your eyes off him. He had those same grey eyes, deep and beautiful like Jay had. He had taken my features and was very fair. He had Yash's talent to write and Jay's ability to be good at everything. He was very young to be good at everything, but he had this will in him, which made him a success at everything. Most importantly, he had this aura and charm around him which made it impossible for people to not love him, and this he had definitely got from Jay.

I still loved Jay, but then I had never let Yash know this. We were married, but he stayed by his words; he never even touched me. I guess he knows that I still love Jay. Pretty evident, eh?

Even today I wonder how Jay must have reacted when he came to know I married Yash. I hadn't talked to him for seven long years. How much I crave to just hear his voice. I would die just to see him. I hadn't looked into those eyes of his for seven long and dreary years. I hadn't felt him, his warmth . . .

Ah! I miss him so much even now, but I restrain myself from even talking to him on the phone when he calls to talk to Ayaan and Yash because I know the effect his voice will have on me. All my will and all my efforts of moving on which I have put in these seven years will be gone down the drain, and I will no longer be able to hold myself back.

It was time to pick Ayaan up, so I had gone to his school.

'Hey, handsome, how was your day, huh?' I asked him as he came towards me and hugged me.

'Long and tiring . . . I hate math, Mom I really find it very tedious and boring,' he said, sulking.

Every day I saw Ayaan, each and every habit of his reminded me of Jay. He was similar to Jay in his habits, so similar that I literally find no difference.

'You are my rock star, right? And it's not even like you are bad at it. Then just drag through it for some years, can't you?' I told him.

'Mom, when can I visit Uncle Jay again? He is so super awesome. I love hanging out with him,' he said, taking out that topic out of nowhere.

Yash had taken Ayaan to meet Jay and his parents some two to three weeks ago, and ever since Ayaan came back, he hasn't stopped gushing about his shenanigans with Jay to me and Yash. He is all about *Jay* these days. I feel kinda jealous, but then I ignore the feeling altogether.

'Don't you think you should concentrate on your studies as of now and forget about going back to Pune?' I asked him rhetorically.

He made this sad, innocent puppy-dog face, which melted me, and I said, 'Fine, I'll let you talk to him over the phone as soon as we go home, so pull that face up, smile, and give Momma a tight hug, fast!' I smiled, hugging him.

His happiness meant the world to me, and I was okay with battling against the whole world and fighting against anyone for Ayaan. He was my life; I lived for him. He was the thread to which my life was hanging on to. I lived only for him, and he was the centre of my universe.

My heart still functions half-heartedly, but the miracle is that it still works. Half of it beats for Ayaan, and the other half still sings, still sings, in the hope that Jay, one fine day, will be mine again and we'll be together, always and forever.

'Mom, you promised me you'll make me talk to Uncle Jay!' Ayaan was yelling, jumping from one sofa to another.

'He is the one who has called. You are in luck,' I told him.

I picked up the phone, and making an effort in a very sweet tone, I said, 'Hello, Jay.'

There was a long pause at the other end, and there was silence for five minutes.

Then breaking the silence between us and letting out a sigh, he said in a very cold and icy tone, 'I have not called to talk to you, you monetary bitch. Give the phone to Ayaan, and do me a favour and don't make me hear your voice again.'

He sounded like a lout, raucous person when he spoke; his words had an edge of disgust, and his tone full of abhorrence.

I was quite offended by it and was speechless for a second or so. I had not talked to him after seven years, seven long and painful years. No matter what had happened, I still was more than delighted to just hear his voice after this long wait, and this is his reaction. And by this, he confirmed all my fears of me being just one more notch to his very glamorous belt.

I handed the phone to Ayaan, let them talk and left the hall because I had no intention of falling loose in front of my son, in whose life I was the pillar of strength.

It was six thirty when Yash came in. Giving him a glass of water, I asked, 'So how was your day?'

'Tedious. The marketing people say I should start with Pune and then Bangalore, but I feel the book will get more publicity if I start the marketing campaign from Bangalore,' he said in a very flat tone.

Pune . . . Why Pune? Suddenly, Jay had started interjecting in every aspect of my life these days out of nowhere. The more I tried to avoid him, the more I was being drawn towards him. And the more I tried to despise him, the deeper I fell in love with him.

'Don't worry. Things will be all right, and one thing, just follow your heart, Yash. You are an intelligent man, you'll figure something out,' I said and went back to the kitchen to prepare dinner.

I just told Yash to follow his heart. What if seven years ago I would have done the same? Maybe it would be Jay in Yash's place, and I, Ayaan, and Jay would be a happy—very happy—family. It was not like Ayaan was not getting everything he should get from Yash, but then Yash will never be able to replace Jay in my life—never.

'I heard Jay had called?' Yash asked me while having dinner.

'Er, yeah, he had called,' I said, and I could sense that my face was losing its colour.

'Something wrong . . . ?' Yash was asking when Ayaan started going all gaga over Jay—as usual.

Gobbling up his morsel in a hurry so that he could talk, Ayaan said, 'You know what, Dad? Uncle Jay promised to take me to an amusement and theme park once I go to Pune. He also said that he'll . . .'

I could no longer take any of that, so feigning that I wanted some water, I went into the kitchen.

'What is wrong, Aish? You seem down and pale since the time I came!' Yash asked, coming inside the kitchen, concerned.

'Nothing, Yash, really, it's nothing actually,' I said, trying to get loose from his hold.

'Aish, you still suck at lying, and I know you too well for you to lie to me,' he said and gave me a hug. 'Temme, what is it, babe . . . Just let it out. It is regarding Jay, am I right?'

'H-how did you decipher that, Yash?' I asked him, a bit surprised.

'Only he can make you this restless, Ash. Only he has that power to totally overpower you and your senses and your heart—all three—which are still with him,' he said, looking into my eyes intently, and even now I could see that the actuality that I loved Jay even now pricked him harshly.

I was so embarrassed, yet I was so full of respect and admiration for Yash. I had only dreamed of getting a guy who would love me like this—unconditionally and irrevocably. I even have him in the form of Yash, but look at me, I never loved this guy with the love which he deserved.

Footwear that we wear are sold in air-conditioned showrooms, but vegetables that we eat are sold on the footpath. The people we ignore love us, and the people we love ignore us; now that's what life is.

Yash held my chin in his hands and gently made me look up and said, 'Did he say something to you, love?'

Tears started brimming out of my eyes, and I couldn't look in his eyes. I just nodded, silently just nodded.

'Look up, Aisha, look up this instant and tell me what happened. I can't bear to see you like this. It kills me to see you like this,' he said, almost on the verge of yelling at me.

'He called me a bitch, a monetary bitch,' I said, and word by word, I gave him a replay of everything that happened.

'Babe, how can you let him affect you so much? Not after all these years, sweetheart . . .' he said, caressing my cheeks, stroking my hair, trying to shush me.

'Mom, I want one more serving please!' I heard Ayaan yelling at the top of his voice.

'Don't break in front of him. You are his inspiration, remember that,' he said, and kissing my hair, he went out and served Ayaan.

Yash made complete sense to my brain but not to my heart. My heart longed for Jay. Jay owned my heart, and he literally did. My craving for him made me weak because he was no longer mine. The guy who was the pillar of strength in my life earlier was now the reason of my weakness. Epic, ain't it?

'Are you full, Ayaan?' I asked him coming out, totally back in my composure.

'Yeah, Momma, and now I am tired,' he said, yawning.

'Not now . . . Now hop, skip, and jump and get to your room. Watch some TV for some time, then we'll do your homework together, okay,' I told him and helped him get down the chair.

Yash was about to say something when he shut himself up, and I was pretty sure it was something related to Jay because there was this ghastly look in his eyes. The look in his eyes was literally haunting me. I could feel the pain and sense what he was going through, but I couldn't help him in any way because the reason of the pain itself was me. Since the time I saw that look in his eyes, I feel guilty as I have literally fried him, killed him, and hurt him beyond boundaries. I don't know whether what I did was right or wrong, and I don't know whether this is the right path or I am just treading the old sought one. I have no clue. All I am doing is listening to my heart, which frays every time it hurts someone, and here I was hurting Yash every freaking second of every single day by thinking about Jay all the time.

The next day started with the same Yash and Ayaan leaving with the normal adieu. I was preparing for my meeting with the British clients after they went when my phone rang. It was Yash calling.

'How many times do I tell you not to call while driving, Yash?' I scolded him as it was not even ten minutes since they left, so obviously he was driving.

'Er, ma'am, are you his wife?' An unfamiliar and strange male voice spoke over the other side.

'Yeah, and may I know who you are, and what is his phone doing with you?' I asked inquisitive and a bit puzzled as to what was going on.

'Actually, your husband has met with an accident on the road near SD International School,' spoke that same guy.

My heart stopped beating for a second. I could just hope Ayaan was not there in the car and nothing serious had happened to Yash. My whole body was trembling, and my voice was getting shaky.

In a very stuttering and scared voice, I asked him, 'Is there any small child with him? And is my husband okay?'

'There was no one in the car except your husband, ma'am. And, er, your husband's condition doesn't seem good, ma'am. We have taken him to City Care Hospital, so please go there,' he said.

'I can't thank you enough. Thank you so much, I'll be there,' I said and kept the phone and raced to the hospital.

As soon as I reached the hospital, I zoomed into the doctor's cabin, and the first question I asked him was, 'Will he be okay?'

'You are Yash Singhania's wife, aren't you?' the doctor asked.

'Yeah, and will you please fill me in with the details?' I begged to him.

'His condition was very grave when he came in. He had suffered some really serious head and spine injuries, and there was severe internal bleeding,' he said and sighed.

'His condition *was* serious? What do you mean?' I asked, and my heart was racing like a Ferrari in a Formula 1 racing championship.

'I am sorry to inform you, Mrs Singhania, we tried our best, but we couldn't save him. We are really sorry,' he said and took me for the identification of his body.

First Dad, after that Mom, and now Yash. What is with people I love? Is it necessary for them to die? Why always me? Yash and Ayaan were the only people whom I could call mine, and now boom, strike and one wicket gone. Yash is no more. He is dead, and I am left alone again—once again . . .

I identified the body which was so badly marred in the face that I couldn't even look straight at it. It hurt to see him like that, and the fact that I could never give him the love he deserved literally killed me from the inside.

This guy sacrificed so much for me, and I never loved him truly, never cared for him genuinely, and never let him own me, my soul, my heart, nor my senses. The things which he yearned for were the things I gave to his brother. They were the things I gave to Jay, and I could only imagine how much that must have pricked Yash. Now there was nothing I could do which would make Yash happy; there was nothing I could say which would make Yash happy. He died a death full of pains and sorrow, both physical and emotional.

I had to break this news to Ayaan, but I didn't have the guts to do so. I had to break this news to Jay and his parents as well. I went to pick Ayaan up as usual.

'Hey, Mom, I won that essay competition!' he said, and hugging me tight, he showed me the certificate. 'Dad will be so happy, wouldn't he?'

My poor baby was so happy that Yash will be happy, and he was so excited to show that certificate to Yash. It was now that I realized how important Yash was in his life and how much Ayaan truly loved him. It was his father who died, his guiding light which just went off.

'Ayaan, I need to tell you something. You know Mom and Dad love you more than anything else in the world, right?' I said, caressing him and making him sit on my lap.

'Yeah, and I love you both too,' he said, smiling and hugging me back.

That smile, that cute smile which lit up my world every single time that curve showed up on his face—it was now gonna turn into a sad grimace. I had no clue as to how he would react, and I was pretty scared. Hence, I decided to call Jay and his parents up here before telling him anything.

I reached home and called Jay up. From his tone it seemed he just woke up from a sound and deep sleep.

'H-hello, Jay?' I asked, stuttering.

'Didn't I tell you to not talk to me?' he asked, and his tone still lethal.

'Yash, he is n-no more.' This was all I could and say, and I started giving out hysterical sobs.

I heard the line go dead without any answer from the other side; the line went dead just like Yash went dead . . .

'Mom, when will Dad come back? I want to show him the certificate! Won't he be super thrilled?' he said, and he was so excited that he was literally jumping from one sofa to another.

My sweetheart, my baby, he was so thrilled about it, and he was so eager to see his dad, to see Yash proud of him, but he'll never be able to see Yash again. He'll never be able to hear Yash say 'I'm proud of you, Ayaan' again . . . He was long gone. It was only his body which was with us, but it will soon turn into nothing but ash, and his Ash, which is me—I won't be able to do anything but see him turn into ash.

'Dad is out of town. Wait for some days. Uncle Jay and Grandpa and Granny will come in tomorrow, okay?' I told him fairly in advance.

'Wow, this is super awesomeness! Uncle Jay is coming, wohoo!' he said, with his excitement bursting beyond boundaries.

He had no clue that Yash is dead. I just couldn't tell him that; I just couldn't. The image of Yash's dead body wasn't ready to leave my brain. No matter how hard I tried, it just wasn't going, and every time I saw that sight, unknowingly, a teardrop would come out of my eyes. As the heart grows older, you come into sight even colder than before.

What a strange life it is. It brought me and Yash together when we were completely unknown to each other and separated us when we were the closest to each other.

The next morning, Jay came in with Mom and Dad around. I didn't have it in me to look in his eyes; I didn't have the guts to. He was looking so good, even better than before. He was a ravishing feast for my eyes, and my yearning and craving for him just reached its epitome. I had missed him so much all these years, and he didn't even look at me, not even one single glance.

'Arrangements have been done. We'll finish off the rituals by three today,' Uncle said, and never in my life had

I seen Uncle in a clutter. He was a mess, a complete mess—both he and Auntie.

Jay was in the hall when I went up to him and said, 'I, er, didn't break the news to Ayaan. I thought maybe you'll be able to handle him better.'

He walked up to me and twisting my wrist in a rough manner and pulling me close he said, 'You, bitch. You don't care whom you hurt, do you?'

'Jay, it's hurting me, leave me,' I said, and I was in vast pain due to the grip of his hand as well as words.

'This is nothing in comparison to what I felt when you fucking married my brother. Did you even think about me before marrying him?' he asked, and I could see huge suffering in his eyes.

'It's not like I was not hurt or I am not hurt, Jay! You left me helpless!' I said, my voice literally breaking in the end.

'Screw yourself with your lies, Aisha. All you care for is money. You couldn't marry me so you trapped my brother,' he said this, and shoving me aside, he went inside his room.

I couldn't believe my ears. He thought I did all this for money, and I thought he knew me more than I know myself! How could he even think I would do this for money? The mere thought of it disgusted me to no ends! I wish I could tell him the reason, I wish I could prove my innocence, and I wish I could get back that same old Jay who used to caress me even if just one tear came out of my eyes. But now I was crying buckets, but his hand never came to close the tap.

All the rituals were finished off, and there was grievance in all our hearts as one piece of all our hearts went away with Yash. He was irreplaceable in our lives.

'Mom, who will scold those bad guy and keep the harm away now that Daddy is not here?' he asked innocently when we were going to sleep, and his eyes were moist.

'Ayaan, look up here. Strong boys don't cry! You are my superhero, right?' I said, hugging him.

'I miss Dad. I love him so much,' he said, cuddling with me in my blanket.

'Dad will take care of you from up there. Now he'll be there to keep a watch on you 24/7, and you always have Momma and Uncle Jay and Granny and Grandpa, and we all love you more than anything, sweetheart.'

Jay, in his own way, had told Ayaan about it. He didn't exactly tell him about the car accident, but Ayaan knew Yash was dead. The reason I let Jay tell him was that Ayaan idolized Jay. He literally worshipped him, and Jay has this strange yet sweet quality of calming frayed nerves and consoling people in the best ways possible.

Ayaan was a kid, so he wasn't that affected by Yash's death because he didn't even know really what death meant; he doesn't realize the seriousness because he is just seven. In a way, I was glad he wasn't that affected because he was the one person I couldn't bear to see in pain.

'Yash's will has to be heard, and there are a lot more formalities to be completed. Ayaan and you will have to come to Pune for that,' Jay told me the next morning, and he wasn't even looking at me when he said that, as if I didn't hold even 1 per cent of importance in his life any more.

'Jay, would you mind behaving at least formal when you talk with me? It was you who cancelled the wedding for one freaking business problem, it was you who put me in a situation wherein I was forced to take some grave decisions. Did you even think about me before cancelling the wedding?' I yelled, and the pain could be sensed in my voice. I could no longer take that behaviour; it hurt every single cell in my body. It was as if he blamed me for everything.

'Don't try and put your load of guilt on my head. I had just postponed the wedding. You—' he was saying when I could no longer hold myself back and I kissed him.

We kissed; we kissed passionately. There was an edge to the kiss. Both of us had let out all the frustration, the anger, the pain, the hurt, and the agony we had suffered in these seven years; we let them out on each other.

He looked up at me after the kiss ended, and he seemed in a throbbing ache. He pulled himself away, and sighing, he said, 'Even today you don't care whom you hurt, do you?'

'You hurt me, Jay, even then and even now!' I said and left the room to pack our bags.

I was in a lot of pain, and my heart was still weeping in anguish over Yash but more over Jay and his words. I was in pain, and I wanted to talk it out. The only person who could really stop me from crying and could make me smile was Jay, and he was the very same reason behind the agonizing pain and grief I was suffering right now and suffered for the last seven years.

I trusted him again. After all these years, I still had hope, and I kept believing in the clouds with silver lining, forgetting the breaching of my trust. I gave it back to be breached once more.

I was packing our bags when I found a heart-shaped pendant with a photo of me and Jay together in it. It was the same pendant he had given me the day I had returned to

India from Paris. He had promised me that time that he'll never break this heart—my heart. But look how iconic and ironic life and the people in it can be. They turn out to do exactly the same things they promised they would never do.

'Why are our bags packed? Are we going somewhere, Momma?' Ayaan asked while I was busy finishing off the last-minute packing.

'Yeah, we are leaving for Pune with Uncle Jay in two to three hours,' I said.

Jay's words were still ringing in my ears. It was like a thousand knives of agony tore into my flesh when those words came out of his mouth. He didn't even give me one chance to explain; one damn chance was all I craved.

My heart is broken and is turned inside out, my words are unspoken, my wet and moist eyes are saying all that needs to be said, and my thoughts and feelings were going through and through my head. How dare he say what he said to me? How dare he do what he did to me? How can one guy, just one guy, cause so much sorrow and misery?

I vowed to myself that no matter how much it pained me, no matter how hard it got, and no matter how much it would break me to do that, I was sure as hell gonna stay away, very away, from Jay because if he doesn't understand my silence, he will never understand my words and sure as hell not my love.

'We will land in a minute or so,' Jay said, coming up to my seat.

I ignored him as if no one just spoke. He waited for me to say something.

'Acting as if I don't exist isn't gonna change the fact that you almost killed me with your ruthlessness and heartlessness,' he said and again managed to sting me with his words.

We reached, and I put Ayaan to sleep after making him eat something. The lawyer was called in, and the will was discussed. To be frank, I wasn't a bit interested in how much money I was getting.

While the servants were serving dinner and Ayaan was busy having fun with *his Uncle Jay*, Auntie came up to me, and with concern in her eyes, she said, 'Aisha, now that Yash is gone, how will you live there alone in Bangalore? I think that you will have to stay here only with us.'

'Mom, no, I can't do this. Ayaan has school in there, and our lives are settled there,' I said, trying to reason out her argument.

'Ayaan stays here no matter where you go and no matter what happens. The choice is now yours,' Jay said, intervening in between out of nowhere.

'Jay Singhania, get one thing straight, Ayaan is my child, and he goes wherever I go! He's mine, and I won't let you steal him from me! I am warning you, back off!' I said, and I said this with every ounce of anger, pain, and frustration filled in me.

'Aisha, do whatever you want. Ayaan stays over here,' he said this so coolly and so very calmly and left the room without hearing any other word.

I felt so annoyed. I mean, I was annoyed beyond limits. What right was he exercising on me and Ayaan? Ayaan was my child, and even though Jay was the biological father, he wasn't his father in practical terms, so he has no right to decide what Ayaan does. But I myself wanted to stay here; I wanted to stay somewhere in the vicinity of where Jay lived.

Ayaan was pretty attached to Jay as well, and he needed a father figure in his life. Maybe I should listen to Mom and Jay and just stay here.

It was around 8 p.m. when the doorbell rang, and I found myself facing a person whom I would have never ever in my wildest and the scariest nightmares imagine to turn up on my doorstep. My memories with her faded for good because we didn't really share good ones.

She gave me a cold and hard look and entered.

'Hello, *beta*, come in and have dinner with us,' Mom said and hugged her.

I was just dumbstruck and was astounded beyond limits. What in the hell was she doing here? This is the last place on earth where I would imagine her. We share a very cold relationship; it's like a cold war between us. I don't even wanna remember what had happened the last time we had talked.

'No, Mom, that's not necessary. We already have a plan to go out for dinner,' Jay said, coming out.

Jay was going out for dinner with her? Is it so necessary for him to always kill me with his actions, words, and looks! Ah! He looked as handsome as ever in those black jeans and grey sweater. Why can't I simply get over him? Couldn't he stop looking so attractive? I mean I am trying to get over him, and that really doesn't help!

'I'll be back late, Mom, don't stay up for me. Let's go, Shanaya,' Jay said to her, and he gave me a look and left.

That look quite confused me. It was like he was showing off Shanaya to me. Yeah, yeah, Jay, make me jealous. And he was quite successful in his motives; I could literally feel the blood flushing through my cheeks. My whole freaking body was on fire.

'Mom, will you please tell me what exactly is happening here?' I asked her, and I was on the verge of going insane.

'Jay and Shanaya are seeing each other. Well, I hope he proposes to her soon. She is from the same batch as you and Jay were. You must know her, right?' she asked me very harmlessly.

How would I not know her! She was Shanaya—Shanaya Desai—after all, Jay's ex-girlfriend but present soon-to-be fiancée. Jay had chosen me over her, but now his priorities seem to have changed. The fact that broke my heart was that she and Jay will probably soon get engaged and will also get married some day. She was gonna live my dream—my dream of becoming Mrs Jay Singhania—and I automatically started despising that snooty rich bitch who always stuck her big snout between me and Jay.

'Yeah, Mom, I know her. In fact, I know her pretty well,' I said and left, leaving Mom confused over my hatred for her.

I couldn't sleep the entire night. All I could think of was Jay and Shanaya. If they get married, I won't be able to survive, let alone live. My life will run out of oxygen; it will run out of my Jay.

'Why are you still awake? Waiting for me, eh?' he asked in a mocking tone, and it was quite late when he came in; I was sitting in the hall.

'I was reading . . . Why would I care what time you come home or with whom you go and do what?' I retorted, and my voice had an edge of jealousy.

'Yeah, I can see how much you care. Time doesn't change the fact that no one knows me better than you,' he said, and it was like for one second he seemed so vulnerable, like the old Jay, like my old Jay.

Under all the anger and hatred for me, there was still love, and that look in his eyes clearly explained that. I met his eyes, and it was as though he still my loved me and he still wanted us to be together, to belong to each other, and I knew this was crazy—totally crazy. Jay is like a whirlpool, having a very powerful and full-packed force within himself, and once again, I was on the verge of getting sucked up in him and his love.

'I need to get some sleep, and so do you, Jay. It seems you haven't had a good sleep since eons,' I said, and I swear I could lose my composure any time. I wanted to cry, cry badly, and I wanted Jay to console me, caress me, but most importantly I wanted him to love me.

'Who do you think is the reason behind my state of wakefulness?' he asked, and he held my waist and pulled me close, very close. But then sighing, he left me, left for his room.

Why? Why do I let him affect me so much? Why does he torture me? Why does he have to behave like he is suffering with multiple personality disorder when he talks to me? It's like there are two sides to him or moreover two minds. One mind hates me beyond limits, and the other still loves me beyond limits. And with him, I am getting squashed as his two minds play squash.

I could have been there in his arms. I could have been there in his arms forever, but it still wouldn't have been long enough. I love him. I love him so much, but somehow my love just doesn't seem enough. Somehow this new version of the relationship we share just doesn't seem enough.

'I am gonna take Ayaan out around the city around three. You wanna join in?' Mom asked.

'Mom, go ahead with him. As much as he is mine, he is yours as well. I want you both to spend time alone,' I said, and I knew she wanted it too.

I hadn't seen Jay since morning. Well, I was hoping I could catch a glance of him at least, but he was nowhere to be seen, and it really would feel awkward asking about him to anybody in the house, given our history and our chemistry.

Ayaan and Mom went out by one, and I was all alone in the big house. I had to get out before I drive myself bananas thinking and mulling over the same things again and again. I went out for a walk. Maybe I'll do some shopping as well.

I was in the mall when I bumped straight into someone.

'Whoa! Watch your step, man!' I said.

'Aisha, is that you?' he asked, his eyes bouncy and with amusement on his face.

'Er, yeah, I am. I am sorry, but I don't seem to recognize you,' I said, and it was a bit awkward and embarrassing.

'It's me, Aditya. Remember?' he asked and gave me a huge boyish grin.

Holy shit! The Aditya I knew was not like this. This guy standing in front of me was someone totally different. He had changed so much. He had grown tall but had the same jet-black hair and stormy black eyes. But boy, his overall physique had changed quite a bit. Before he was so skinny, and now his physique could be compared to a gym trainer.

'Oh gosh, I do not believe this! You have changed so much! I mean, I just didn't recognize you for a second. Oh my god, Adi, I swear you've changed,' I exclaimed in surprise.

'You bet I did. But you are still the same, you are still as beautiful as ever, haven't changed a bit,' he said and somewhat reminded me of our past.

Aditya and Jay never really got along well. Well, Aditya nursed feelings for me back then, which obviously didn't go down well with Jay, but Aditya was never that sorta guy who would bother me once he knew I had feelings for Jay.

'So what's up with you, eh?' I asked him.

'Nothing much actually . . . Well, I heard about, er, Yash's death. I wish to express my condolences,' he said, and he was observing me, waiting for my reaction. 'Well, somehow everyone was shocked when they learnt of your marriage with him.'

Well, in the beginning I myself was shocked, I wanted to say. But then I said, 'Hmm. So what about you? Found anyone?'

'Who'd have me?' he said and gave me a dimpled smile.

Yeah, as if, I thought. I looked around the mall and half a dozen gals were staring or, better word, gawking at him—some secretly, some openly, and some shyly. He was like a magnet for all gals with his good looks and manly physique and not to forget his stormy eyes. He attracted everyone, and it was very apparent that all eyeballs stuck to him.

'Yeah right, liar . . . Let's go and grab something to eat? I am starving,' I said, and we left for a coffee shop.

I ate like a famine victim, but time passed in catching up with him, and it was already six when we got up to leave. Time went by in a spur.

'Now that I have your number, I'll make sure we don't lose touch,' he said and gave me a goodbye hug. There was something more from his side in that hug; there was definitely something more.

I was still thinking over it when I reached home. I entered, and I saw Jay sleeping harmlessly on the couch. It reminded me of those good old days. He still looked so innocent and vulnerable in his sleep, so defenceless. I wish I could protect him; I wish I could hug him.

'Where had you been?' he demanded, getting up from the couch.

I didn't find myself liable to answer that, but just so I could talk to him, I said, 'Mom and Ayaan have gone out to the park, so I went shopping, and guess what, I bumped into Aditya. It was so good meeting him after all these years. We caught up over a cup of coffee . . .' I said, giving him an innocent smile.

'Aditya who? Joshi?' he asked.

I nodded.

'Why would you have coffee with him?' he asked, and he seemed quite upset over the fact that I did.

'I know you and Adi didn't get along well, but it's the past, and he is a pretty decent guy,' I said, defending myself as well as Aditya.

He came closer to me and twisted my hand, and bringing me close, he said, 'Don't you dare go out with him again.'

'Excuse me? Jay, you have no right to hold me like this, and nor do you have the right to stop me from meeting him or anyone else for that matter!' I said, and I was quite taken aback by his harshness.

'I have got every right. Show me what you got, bitch! He got money, eh?' he said, and his eyes showed jealousy and hatred.

I struck him hard on his face and yelled, 'I do not love people because of money, and get that fucking thing straight!'

'Then why would you fucking marry Yash, Aisha? Gimme one good reason! You couldn't wait for me to come back? Is that how serious your love was for me? Couldn't get into my bank account, so you married my brother?' he said, and with every word, there was agony dripping from it.

'Heck you didn't leave me any other option, and he asked me to marry him. He gave me support when I needed it!' I said in tears.

'To hell with your options, Aisha! Did you even once think, just once, before marrying Yash? Didn't you even once think what will happen to me without you?' he said, and I could see he was in pieces, literal pieces.

'I loved you so much, but you didn't even think twice before cancelling the wedding and flying off to New York! It broke me, it killed me,' I said, and I wished he would come and hold me.

'Did it even kill your love for me?' he asked.

I was not going to answer that. He knew I loved him, and I still do, but still he was asking me that. I couldn't give him a confirmation. No, I wouldn't. He was waiting for me to say something, but I didn't have anything.

'Say something, goddamit, say something, Aisha! Temme you love me because I can see that in your eyes!' he bellowed, and he held me; he held me in his arms.

I wish I could say I love you, but there was no voice coming out of my throat. My phone rang perfectly at the wrong time and ruined things.

'Y-yeah, Mom . . . ?' I asked, not really trusting my voice.

I collapsed right there after hearing what she had to say. The phone slid away from my hands. He panicked and asked, 'What's wrong, Aish? What happened! Tell me what happened before I go mad!' he said, and he was pretty shaken up too.

'We need to go. Ayaan is in the hospital, he met with an accident,' I said, and as soon as the words were out of my mouth, I and Jay were out of the house.

He drove like a maniac, but I just didn't care. I was numb—just numb and lifeless. If anything happened to Ayaan, I swear I would kill myself—literally kill myself. He is my life; he is everything I live for. He has to be all right; nothing can happen to him. We reached the hospital, and I rushed in.

'Mom, please tell me nothing's wrong, please!' I begged to her.

'Nothing is wrong, but he'll need some blood as he has lost blood, and he'll need the blood soon,' she said, and she looked dead and pale.

'Where's the doctor? I wanna talk to him,' Jay asked. 'Let's go.'

He held my hand as we went inside the doctor's cabin, and I didn't object. I needed it.

'Ayaan Singhania is my child. Would you please tell me exactly what has happened?' I asked him, and I was still not convinced that everything is okay. I had this gut feeling that something major is gonna take place.

'Ah, yes. His condition isn't that serious. Things will be very fine soon, but due to the loss of blood, we need a blood backup soon to give him,' the doctor said.

'So give him the blood,' Jay said in a dominating tone.

'Er, sir, he has a rare blood group which is not available in the blood bank. So if any of you could donate?' he asked.

My face was losing its colour. I was A+ and Yash was B+, but Ayaan was O- and Jay was O- as well . . .

'So what is his blood group?' Jay asked, now annoyed. He loved Ayaan a lot too; he couldn't bear this either.

'Well, sir, he is O-. If any one of you is O negative, the process will ease off,' the doctor said.

Jay was astounded by what he heard. He looked at me but said nothing. He took time to digest the information. But then said, 'Well, I surprisingly happen to be of the same blood group, so hurry up and take my blood. I am ready to donate.' His countenance was straight; he showed no emotions on his face.

'Right away, sir . . .' the doctor said and led him to some room while I was asked to be seated in the waiting room.

I wondered what must be going through Jay's head at the moment. He isn't that stupid to not understand what this meant. I was afraid of confronting him; no, I didn't want to. I had lied to him about Ayaan, and he had as good as found out about it. What will this news result into? That is what I am more afraid of.

Mom had gone home for some time. He came out after, let's say, forever. I feared this moment; I had no energy to face him. I had to face him. It was not a choice; it was a necessity.

He came up to me and held my hand. Then with intense gentleness, he asked, 'Why does Ayaan's blood group match mine and not Yash's blood group?'

'H-how would I know? You never know how deep genes can get,' I said, stammering out my words.

'Is Ayaan my son? Aisha, answer me honestly!' he said very firmly yet tenderly, caressing my hand.

'Yes, Jay, he is your son! You got me pregnant and left for New York! This is the reason why I said you left me with no other option!' I said, and I was shaking and crying. All the emotions which had been buried deep inside were coming out. They came out after seven dreary and long years.

He took me close, and he simply hugged me. Moaning, he said, 'Aish, you could have told me this and I would have left everything and I would have come running to you. I loved you so much that I would have literally begged you to marry me.'

'W-what about now? You don't love me any more, do you?' I asked him.

'Why do you think did I get so jealous when you mentioned Aditya? Why do you think these many years I didn't get married to anyone? That was because my heart was with you, because I loved you, Aisha Mukherjee, and I love you with the same intensity even today, even now . . .'

'Shanaya . . . ?' I asked faintly.

'She was just a date. We went to some parties together, and Mom imagined me dating her. You know how Mom is, sweetheart, don't you?' he asked me lovingly, and how much I had craved such love from him, how much I longed to belong to him.

All I wanted was to be needed by him, to be important and indispensable to him. I was addicted to him; it was a mutual addiction. It was faith in my love for him and my love for Ayaan that kept me alive for these many years; it was what made my life worth living.

'You have no clue as to how much I love you and how much I missed you. Yash married me only for Ayaan, we never shared that kinda relationship. It was always you whom I loved, and it will always be so . . .' I said, and I rested my head on his shoulder.

The happiness I saw in his eyes when I said those words, it couldn't be compared to anything. It was worth a million dollars—that smile. That smile itself was a proof to how much Jay loved me.

'I have been waiting for what seems like infinity to be with you and to get beyond my boundaries and limitations, but with you, I know can begin. I love you, Aish, and I wanna spend my whole life with you. Time ceases to be a measure when I am with you, but let's just say we'll start with forever. Marry me, Aisha,' he said those words, and he kissed me, a light one.

Those words meant the world to me. The world will be balanced when we are balanced, and we become balanced when we find someone who completes us in ways more than one and this guy in front of me completed me in every way possible.

In a way, the reason that all this happened was me, and Jay loved me even after all this. The wrong kind of people hate us for the good in us, but the right kind of people love us even after knowing the bad in us, and now I was finally getting my Mr Right.

'I will marry you, Jay. I missed you so much all these years. It was so difficult to stay without you. It was a life full of pains and sufferings, but I never stopped loving you. I love you, a lot more than you know, more than you'll ever know.'

We had overcome all the obstacles and hurdles life had put in front of us. We passed them with flying colours, and now finally, our souls were entwining again to be together and to continue in our small blissful piece called forever. Now we were gonna be together . . . Together, always and forever.